There was a gorgeous, almost naked woman in his bed

Max woke to find himself curled around Maddy, her rear nestled into the cradle formed by his hips and thighs. One of his arms was wrapped around her torso. Her hair was everywhere, streaming across the pillow, across his shoulder and arm.

He was painfully hard, his erection pressed against the roundness of her backside. His hand somehow crept beneath her T-shirt to rest just below the lower curve of her breasts.

God, she felt good. Small and sleek and feminine.

He wanted to flex his hips and grind himself against her so badly it hurt. His whole body tensed as he imagined sliding his hand up a few vital inches and cupping her breast. He could almost feel the softness of it beneath his hand.

He closed his eyes. He had to back off. Now.

Then Maddy stirred, her body flexing in his embrace, her backside snuggling closer to his hips.

He'd never been so close to losing control in his life.

Blaze

Dear Reader,

This is (hopefully) the only book in my career that I will ever have to write twice. I'm still not quite sure how it happened, but the whole of the almost-completed manuscript for *Amorous Liaisons* was swallowed by my computer just before Christmas 2007—and I didn't have a backup. Much gnashing of teeth and hair pulling and desperate sobbing later, I sat down to start writing again.

Fortunately I had the first three chapters in a separate file, and I knew exactly what needed to happen because, well, I'd already written the book once. It was hard, and there were times when I was desperate for this book to be finished, but I am now also pretty proud of myself for completing it. Is it the same as the first version? I will never know. Is it a satisfying, emotional read? I hope you think so—it was certainly a satisfying, emotional write.

I did a lot of research into retired ballet dancers before I wrote this book and I was constantly moved by their stories. When you become passionate about something at four years old, having to leave it behind at thirty is a real blow. I truly felt Maddy's pain as I wrote, and I hope her story resonates with you.

I love hearing from readers. You can contact me via my Web site www.sarahmayberryauthor.com, or via snail mail at Harlequin Enterprises Ltd., 225 Duncan Mill Road, Toronto, ON M3B 3K9, Canada.

Happy reading,

Sarah Mayberry

AMOROUS LIAISONS
Sarah Mayberry

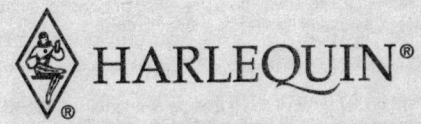

TORONTO • NEW YORK • LONDON
AMSTERDAM • PARIS • SYDNEY • HAMBURG
STOCKHOLM • ATHENS • TOKYO • MILAN • MADRID
PRAGUE • WARSAW • BUDAPEST • AUCKLAND

If you purchased this book without a cover you should be aware that this book is stolen property. It was reported as "unsold and destroyed" to the publisher, and neither the author nor the publisher has received any payment for this "stripped book."

ISBN-13: 978-0-373-79429-4
ISBN-10: 0-373-79429-0

AMOROUS LIAISONS

Copyright © 2008 by Small Cow Productions PTY Ltd.

All rights reserved. Except for use in any review, the reproduction or utilization of this work in whole or in part in any form by any electronic, mechanical or other means, now known or hereafter invented, including xerography, photocopying and recording, or in any information storage or retrieval system, is forbidden without the written permission of the publisher, Harlequin Enterprises Limited, 225 Duncan Mill Road, Don Mills, Ontario M3B 3K9, Canada.

This is a work of fiction. Names, characters, places and incidents are either the product of the author's imagination or are used fictitiously, and any resemblance to actual persons, living or dead, business establishments, events or locales is entirely coincidental.

This edition published by arrangement with Harlequin Books S.A.

® and TM are trademarks of the publisher. Trademarks indicated with ® are registered in the United States Patent and Trademark Office, the Canadian Trade Marks Office and in other countries.

www.eHarlequin.com

Printed in U.S.A.

ABOUT THE AUTHOR

Sarah Mayberry has moved eight times in the past five years and is currently living in New Zealand—although that may change at the drop of a hat. When she's not moving house or writing, she loves to read, go to the movies, buy shoes and travel (mostly to find more shoe shops). She has been happily partnered to her man for over fifteen years, and plans to make it many more.

Books by Sarah Mayberry
HARLEQUIN BLAZE
211—CAN'T GET ENOUGH
251—CRUISE CONTROL*
278—ANYTHING FOR YOU*
314—TAKE ON ME**
320—ALL OVER YOU**
326—HOT FOR HIM**
380—BURNING UP
404—BELOW THE BELT

*It's All About Attitude
**Secret Lives of Daytime Divas

Don't miss any of our special offers. Write to us at the following address for information on our newest releases.

Harlequin Reader Service
U.S.: 3010 Walden Ave., P.O. Box 1325, Buffalo, NY 14269
Canadian: P.O. Box 609, Fort Erie, Ont. L2A 5X3

Bless you, Chris, for your enormous sympathy and patience with me as I grieved, anguished and swore over this book. I love you very much.

To Wanda, for being so calm and supportive and damned smart as always—every time you make me lift my game, and this time you had your work cut out for you.

And to my friends and family who all made sympathetic noises and passed the chocolate at the right times. Where would I be without you?

1

MADDY GREEN was finding it hard to breathe. She lengthened her stride, eager to reach the rehearsal studio. She could almost feel the familiar smoothness of the barre beneath her hand and almost see the glint of bright lights in the mirrors and hear the regular scuff and thump of other dancers leaping and landing and twisting and turning around her.

She needed the comfort of the familiar very badly right now.

The double doors to the Sydney Dance Company's rehearsal studio A came up on her left. She pushed through them and the scent of warm bodies, clean sweat and a dozen different deodorants and perfumes and aftershaves wrapped itself around her.

Home. She was home.

"Maddy! How did your doctor's appointment go?" Kendra asked the moment she spotted Maddy.

The other dancers turned toward her, faces expectant. Maddy forced herself to smile and shrug casually.

"It's all good," she said. "No problems."

She couldn't bring herself to say the other thing. Saying it out loud would make it real. And for just a few more minutes, she wanted to lose herself in the world that had held her enthralled since, at the age of four, she first saw a picture of a ballerina.

Kendra flew across the room to give her a hug, her slender arms strong around Maddy's back.

"Fantastic. Great news. The best," she said.

The other woman's gauzy rehearsal skirt flared around her legs as she returned to her place in the center of the room. Kendra was only twenty-two. She had her whole career ahead of her. She was a beautiful dancer—powerful, delicate, emotional, intense. She would soar.

Maddy felt someone watching her and lifted her gaze to find Stephen Jones, the choreographer, eyeing her closely.

She turned her shoulder, breaking the contact. Stephen had been watching her a lot lately, checking her range of movement, testing the capabilities of her injured knee. Had he known, or guessed, what she'd been told today? Had everyone known except her that she was over? That she would never dance again?

Her heart pounded against her ribs and again she couldn't quite catch her breath.

She threw her bag into the corner and slid off her street shoes, bending to tug on a pair of slippers with shaking hands. The ribbons whispered through her fingers as she wrapped them around her ankles and tied them neatly. She shed her skirt to reveal tights and leotard and took a place at the barre to begin warming up.

Pliés first, then some *rond de jambes,* keeping her head high and her arms relaxed. Every time she rose up *en pointe,* she felt the seamless, fluid glide of her body responding to her will, saw her reflection in the floor-to-ceiling mirror, posture perfect, form ideal.

Her heartbeat slowed. She was a dancer. Always had been, always would be.

"Maddy."

She tore her eyes from her own reflection to find Andrew McIntyre, the company director, standing behind her. He, too, had been studying her perfect form in the mirror.

"Why don't you come to my office?" he said. His voice was gentle, as was the light in his eyes.

He knew.

He'd spoken to Dr. Hanson. Of course he had. Hanson was the company's doctor, after all. When she'd come on board four years ago she'd signed a contract agreeing that the company could access all health matters pertaining to her career.

"After rehearsal," she said. "I'm warm now. And the rest of them are waiting for me."

"I think we should do this now, don't you?" he said.

He was frowning, as though what she'd said pained him in some way. He moved closer, reached out a hand to touch her.

She took a step backward. Rising *en pointe* on her bad leg, she lifted her right leg in *grand battement* to the side then up, up, up, until her toe was pointing toward the ceiling, her thigh straight beside her ear.

She held the position in a blatant display of skill and strength, her eyes daring Andrew in the mirror.

He held her gaze, never once looking away. And when her muscles began to scream and shake from the pain of holding such a demanding, strenuous position, he stepped forward and rested his hand on her shoulder.

"Enough, Maddy. Come to my office."

She let her leg drop and relaxed onto her flat feet. Her knee throbbed, as it always did these days when she demanded too much of it. She hung her head and stared blindly at the polished floorboards.

She felt Andrew slide his arm around her shoulders. Then he led her toward the door. The other dancers stopped mid-rehearsal to watch her. She could feel their silent stares as she and Andrew stepped into the corridor. Andrew didn't let her go until they were in his office.

"Sit," he said.

He crossed to the wooden built-ins that spanned one wall of his office and opened a door. She heard the clink of glass on glass as he poured something.

"Drink this."

Brandy fumes caught her nose as he lifted a glass to her lips.

"No," she said, turning her head away.

Andrew held the glass there, waiting. Finally she took a token mouthful.

"And again," he said.

She took a bigger mouthful this time. The brandy burned all the way down her throat to her belly. She shook her head firmly when he offered a third time.

He took her at her word and placed the glass on the coffee table in front of her. Then he sat in the armchair opposite her.

In his late fifties, he was a former dancer, his body slim and whippet-strong even after years away from the stage. His tanned skin was stretched tightly across high cheekbones, and thin lines surrounded his mouth from smoking. His eyes were kind as he studied her, a rarity from a man who was known throughout the dance world as a perfectionist first and a human being second.

"We will look after you, Maddy. Please know that. Retirement pay, any teaching work you want—you name it, you can have it. You've been one of our greatest dancers, and we won't forget you."

Maddy could feel the sweat cooling on her body in the air-conditioned chill.

"I want to keep dancing," she said. "That's what I want."

Andrew shook his head decisively. "You can't. Not for us. Not professionally. Your spirit might be willing, but your body is not. Dr. Hanson was very clear about that. We always knew that complete recovery from such a significant tear to your cruciate ligament was going to be a long shot. It's time to hang up your slippers, Maddy."

She stared at him, a storm of words closing her throat.

Anger, grief, resentment, denial—she didn't know what to say, how to react.

"I want to keep dancing," she said again. "Give me more time. I'll show you I can do it. I'll do more rehab work, more Pilates. Whatever it takes."

Andrew's face went slack for a moment, and he leaned back and closed his eyes, rubbing the bridge of his nose with his hand. He looked defeated, sad.

"Maddy. I know how hard it is to give it up. Believe me. It nearly killed me. But I made a second chance for myself." He paused a moment to let his words sink in. "You're a beautiful, smart, resourceful woman. There's another life out there waiting for you. You just have to find it."

I don't want to find it.

She almost said it out loud, but some of the numbness and shock were leaving her as the brandy burned its way into her system.

The doctor had handed down his decision, and Andrew had made his, too. She was broken, old. They had no use for her anymore.

"We'll throw you a party. A real send-off. And we'll help you any way we can. Retraining, or, as I said earlier, if you want to teach…?"

The thought of a party, of standing in front of her peers while people made toasts to her former talent made bile rise up the back of her throat.

"No. No party," she said.

Suddenly she didn't want to be here anymore. When the doctor had given her the news an hour ago, the company had felt like home, like the safe place to be. But now she knew it would never be her home again.

"People will want to say their goodbyes, pay their due respects," he said.

"I'm not dead," she said, standing abruptly.

She strode to the door. She hesitated for a beat outside the rehearsal studio, then braced herself to duck in and collect her bag. Head down, she did just that, not responding when Kendra asked if she was okay.

They would hear soon enough. Another dancer would be promoted into her role in the latest production. Maybe Kendra. Maybe one of the other soloists. Life would go on.

Outside in the warm summer air, she took deep breaths and fought tears.

She had never been more alone and scared in her life. Her entire world had crumbled around her—the discipline and passion that had formed the boundaries of her days and nights had dissolved into nothingness. She had no future, and her past was irrelevant. She was the owner of a broken body and broken dreams and precious little else.

She found her car keys in her handbag, but she had nowhere to go. No current lover to offer his shoulder, and no former lovers to call on, because her affairs never ended well. Her mother was miles away in America, enjoying the fruits of her third marriage. Maddy had never known her father. All her friends were dancers, and the thought of their ready sympathy had the bile rising in her throat again.

Where to go?

Where to go?

Out of the depths of her subconscious, a face rose up. Clear gray eyes, dark hair, a smile that offered mischief and fun and comfort and understanding in equal measure.

Max.

Yes. She needed Max. Even though it had been years. Even though their friendship had been reduced to occasional e-mails and Christmas cards.

He would understand. He always had. He'd hold her in his big, solid arms, and she'd feel safe, the way she always had with him.

And then maybe she could think. Imagine a world without dance. Construct a way forward.

Max.

MAX SHUT THE FLAP on the box and held it down with his forearm. He reached for the packing tape and used his thumbnail to find the leading edge.

"I'm all done in here. How about you?" a voice asked from the doorway.

He glanced up at his sister, Charlotte, taking in her smug expression and the way she'd planted her hands on her hips.

"Don't even think it," he said, tearing off a piece of tape and sticking the flap down.

"My room's finished. Technically, that means my work here is done," Charlotte said.

Max tossed her the spare roll of packing tape. So far, he'd only managed to pack away half of the books in his late father's extensive collection.

"The sooner you start helping, the sooner we can both get out of here," he said.

Charlotte propped herself against the door frame.

"Should have picked an easier room, Max," she teased.

"I was being gallant. Giving you the kitchen and taking on this Herculean task to save you hours of hard labor. In case you hadn't noticed."

Charlotte's smile faded a little as she straightened.

"Where do you want me to start?" she asked.

Max glanced at the solid wall of books that remained unpacked.

"Pick a shelf. Any shelf," he said.

Charlotte busied herself assembling a box as he started stacking books into another carton.

Dust hung in the air, dancing in the weak winter sunlight filtering through the dirty windows of his father's apartment.

It felt strange to be back here, and yet he'd only been gone two months. The whole world had shifted in that time.

His father was dead.

He still couldn't quite believe it. Ten weeks ago, Alain Laurent had succumbed to a bout of pneumonia, a constant hazard for quadriplegics. After a week-long battle, he'd died quietly in his sleep. Max had been out of the room, taking a phone call at the time. After eight years of constant care and devotion, after being there for so many of the major crises of his father's illness, Max had missed the most important moment of all.

Had his father known that he was alone? Or, as his sister contended, had his father chosen that moment to slip away for good, sparing his son the anguish of witnessing his final moments?

"Stop giving yourself a hard time," Charlotte said from across the room.

He frowned. "What?"

"You heard me. Don't pretend you weren't sitting there, thinking about Dad again. You did everything you could. We both did," Charlotte said firmly.

He made a dismissive gesture and packed more books.

"It's true, you know. What you just said. You are gallant. Which is charming on one level, but bloody infuriating on another."

He smiled at his sister's choice of words. They were half-Australian, half-French, but he always thought of Charlotte as being essentially European, with her dark hair and elegant fashion sense. Then, out of the blue, she'd toss out a bit of Aussie slang and remind him that they'd spent their teen years in Sydney, Australia, swimming and surfing and swatting flies away from backyard barbecues.

"I'm serious, Max," she said. "You're always riding to the

rescue, thinking of everyone else except yourself. You need to learn to be selfish."

He made a rude noise and continued to work.

"The day you think of yourself first, I'll give it a go."

Charlotte pushed her hair behind her ear, frowning. "That's different. I have a family. I gave up the right to be selfish when I became a parent."

Max dropped the book he was holding and pressed a hand to his heart. Moving with a quarter of his former grace and skill, he half staggered, half danced to the side wall, playing self-sacrifice and martyrdom for all he was worth.

"Very funny," his sister said.

He dodged the small book she flung his way.

He tossed the book back and she shook her head at him. They packed in silence for a few beats, busy with their own thoughts.

He wondered who was looking after Eloise and Marcel today, Charlotte's children with her merchant banker husband, Richard. He knew Charlotte was between babysitters at the moment. It was hard finding people competent to deal with Eloise's special needs, but having them here hadn't really been possible. Any disruption to Eloise's routine inevitably led to distress.

"I never really thanked you, did I?" Charlotte said into the silence.

He pushed the flaps shut on another full box of books. The secondhand dealer was going to have a field day with their father's collection. Everything from 1960s dime-store novels to Proust and Dante.

"That's because there's nothing to thank me for."

"Do you miss it? Dancing?" Charlotte asked quietly.

He started assembling another box.

"Sometimes. Not so much anymore. It's a long time ago now."

"Only eight years. Perhaps you could—"

"No," he said, more sharply than he'd intended. "Eight years is a lifetime in dance, Charlie. I'm too old now. Lost my flexibility, my edge."

And he'd moved on, too. When the call had come through eight years ago that his father had been in a car accident, Max had flown straight from Sydney to Paris in the hope that he'd be able to say goodbye before nature took its course. As it turned out, he'd had eight years to say his goodbyes.

As soon as it became apparent that their father would survive his injuries but be confined to a wheelchair, Max had made the changes necessary to ensure his father's comfort. He'd resigned from the avant-garde Danceworks company where he'd been earning himself a name in Australia and arranged to have his belongings shipped to Paris. Then he had moved into his father's apartment in the genteel, refined arrondissement of St. Germain and started the renovations that had made it possible for him to care for his father at home.

It hadn't been an easy decision and there had been moments—especially at the very beginning when he and his father had been acclimating to their new roles—when Max had bitterly regretted his choices. He'd left so much behind. His career, his dreams, his friends. The woman he loved.

But Alain Laurent had been a generous and affectionate parent. When their mother had died when Max was ten years old and Charlotte just eight, Alain had done everything in his power to ensure they never felt the lack of a mother's love. He had been a man in a million, and for Max there had never been any doubt that he and Charlotte would do whatever was necessary to make the remainder of his life as rewarding as possible.

"You could have left it to me. Thousands of men would have," Charlotte said.

"On behalf of my gender, I thank you for your high opinion of us," he said drily.

"You know what I mean."

He stopped and faced his sister.

"Let's put this to bed, once and for all. I did what I wanted to do, okay? He was my father, too. I loved him. I wanted to care for him. I couldn't have lived with it being any other way. Just as you couldn't have lived with having to choose between Richard and your children and Dad. End of story."

Charlotte opened her mouth then shut it again without saying anything.

"Good. Can we move on now?"

Charlotte shrugged. Then, slowly, she smiled. "I'd forgotten how bossy you can be. It's been a while since you read me the riot act."

"Admit it, you miss it," he said, glad she'd dropped the whole gratitude thing.

Of course, willingly supporting his father didn't stop the what-ifs from leaking out of his subconscious in the unguarded moments before falling asleep at night.

What if he'd been able to follow his dream and dance in London, New York, Moscow, Paris? Would he have made it, achieved soloist status and seen his name in lights?

And what would have happened with Maddy? Would he ever have told her how he felt? How much he loved her—and not just as her reliable friend and sometime dancing partner?

As always when he thought of Maddy, he pictured her on stage, standing in a circle of light, her small, elegant body arched into a perfect arabesque. Then came the memories of her as a woman, laughing with him on the ratty couch in the dump of a house they'd shared with two other dancers, or lounging on the back porch in the hot evening air.

False memories, he knew. Gilded by time and distance. Maddy couldn't possibly be as funny, as warm and beautiful and sensual as he remembered her. He'd turned her into a symbol of everything he'd given up.

"So, what are you going to do now?" Charlotte asked as she slid a box across the worn parquetry floor to join the others he'd stacked against the wall.

He deliberately misunderstood her.

"Finish packing these boxes, then find someplace warm to have a cold demi of beer," he said.

She rolled her eyes. "I mean next. What are you going to do now that you've got your life back?"

He shrugged, even as his thoughts flew to the apartment he'd rented in the Marais district across the river. His sister hadn't seen it yet. It had been hell holding her off, and he would have to tell her his plans soon, but he wasn't ready for her disapproval yet. He was still coming to terms with his own audacity himself.

"I haven't really thought about it," he lied.

Charlotte dusted her hands on her butt. "Well, you should. You could use Dad's money to go to university, get a degree. Or put a deposit on a place of your own. Start making a life for yourself. Hell, you could even get a girlfriend. Really shake things up."

It was Max's turn to roll his eyes. "Why is it that married people always think that everyone else would be happier in a relationship?"

"Because it's true. And you're made to be a husband, Max. If any man should have children, it's you. They'd be gorgeous, for starters. And talented. And smart and kind."

"Why does it sound like you're writing copy for a personals ad?"

"Relax. I haven't stooped that low. Yet. But I do have some wonderful friends I'd love you to meet."

"No."

"Why not? Give me one good reason why you don't want to meet an attractive, available woman?"

"I'll find my own woman when I'm ready." The truth was,

the next twelve months were going to be challenging enough without adding a new relationship into the mix.

"For God's sake. Surely you must want the sex, at the very least? How many years can a man survive on hand relief alone, anyway?" Charlotte asked.

He nearly choked on his own tongue. Half amused, half surprised, he stared at his sister. She was many things, but comfortable with earthy talk was not one of them.

"*Hand relief?* Are you serious?"

"What's a better word for it? Happy ending? Spanking the monkey? Choking the chicken?"

He laughed because he couldn't help himself. "Are you done yet?"

"Max, I'm serious," Charlotte said.

He saw with surprise that there were tears in her eyes. "Look, your concern for my…um…monkey is sweet. I think. But I'm not going to discuss my sex life with my sister."

"That's because you don't have one. And it's such a waste, Max. I know women who would crawl over broken glass to get to you. Let me hook you up with one of them."

He held up a hand. "Spare me the broken-glass crawlers. Please. And take my word for it that I have a sex life."

He thought of Marie-Helen and Jordan, women he'd slept with on a casual basis over the years. He liked them both, he enjoyed the sex, but he was not compelled by either woman. That lack of engagement had been important in his former life, when all his energy had been focused on his father's well-being.

"Well. I hope that's true." Charlotte studied his face. "I want you to have all the things you've missed out on."

"I get that. Thank you," he said. "Now, can we talk about something else? Anything else, in fact. Global warming? The extortionate price of tropical fruit?"

Charlotte let the subject go. They spent another two hours

boxing up the library. By the time they exited the apartment, they were both dusty and weary.

"What time are you letting the dealer in tomorrow?" he asked.

"Around ten."

They both stood on the threshold, glancing around the apartment that had been their father's home, hospital and prison.

"Will you miss it?" she asked.

The apartment had been in their family for two generations. He could remember his grandmother serving Sunday meals in the dining room, the family gathered around. But he could remember more clearly his father's pain and suffering.

"No. You?"

She shook her head. "Too many sad memories."

He locked up for the last time and handed the key to his sister. They parted ways in the street and he walked two blocks to the Metro. After changing lines twice, he climbed the stairs of the St. Paul station and emerged into the weak afternoon sunlight.

It was early February, and he could see his breath in the air. He stopped to buy a bottle of wine and some fresh-baked bread on his way home. Then he let himself into the former shop that he'd leased on a cobblestoned side street of Le Marais.

His footsteps echoed as he made his way across a wide expanse of floorboards to the kitchen.

Normally a place the size of his loft would cost a mint to rent, but he'd managed to discover the last shitty, unrenovated hole in the upwardly mobile third arrondissement. What it lacked in ambience, hygiene and plumbing it gained in space. More than enough to accommodate his bed, a couch, an armchair, a kitchen table and all his workshop materials and leave him with plenty of room to fill with his art.

His art.

He studied the handful of small sculptures and the one full-size figure in bronze that stood next to his workbench.

For a long time he'd fooled himself into thinking that his sketches and small-scale sculptures were a hobby, mindless doodling to chew up the time between tending to his father's needs and fill the hole that losing dancing had left. He'd always drawn and experimented with clay, ever since he was a kid. It was harmless, he'd figured, pointless.

But as his skill had increased, so had his drive to capture more and more of his ideas in clay, plaster, bronze—each time bigger and better than the time before. He'd pushed away the urge as it became more insistent, but when his father's health had deteriorated a few months ago, he'd found himself thinking about what would happen after his father had found his peace. Max's hands had itched as he imagined what he could do with his art if he had more time, more space, more energy.

The past eight years had taught him that life was never predictable, often cruel, and even more often capricious. Men plan and God laughs—he'd often thought the quote should be men *dream* and God laughs.

But he'd had a gutful of what-ifs. He'd had eight years of being on hold, in limbo, living for someone else.

He and Charlotte had inherited a small sum of money from their father's estate. There would be a little more when the apartment sale was finalized—but not much since they'd taken out a mortgage to fund their father's care—and Max had decided to recklessly, perhaps foolishly, use his share to give himself a year to prove himself. The rent paid, food supplied, his materials purchased. And if he had nothing to show for it at the end of it all, so be it. At least he would have followed one of his dreams through to its conclusion.

His hands and face felt grubby from the hours amongst dusty books. He stripped and took a quick shower. His hair damp, clad in a pair of faded jeans and a cashmere sweater that had seen better days, he slit the seal on the merlot he'd bought and placed a single glass on the counter.

The sound of his doorbell echoed around the loft. He eyed the distant front door cautiously.

He wouldn't put it past Charlotte to pay a sneak visit after the conversation they'd had today, trying to catch him in the act of having a sex life so she could truly rest easy.

He ran his hands through his hair. His sister was going to find out her brother was chasing a rainbow sometime. Might as well be today.

His bare feet were silent as he made his way to the white-painted glass front door. He could see a small silhouette on the other side of the glass and he frowned. Too short for Charlotte. And too slight for either Jordan or Marie-Helen.

He twisted the lock and pulled the door open.

And froze when he saw who was standing on his doorstep.

"Maddy."

"Max," she said.

Then she threw herself into his arms.

2

MADDY PUSHED HERSELF away from Max's embrace and brushed the tears from the corners of her eyes. He appeared utterly blown away to see her. She suddenly realized how stupid she must seem, arriving on his doorstep unannounced and crying all over him.

She was feeling kind of blown-away herself. It had been eight years since she'd last seen his face, and she was surprised at how much older and grown-up he seemed. He was thirty-one now, of course. No longer a young man. She hadn't expected him to remain untouched by time, but the reality of him was astonishing. He almost looked like a stranger, with new lines around his mouth and eyes. His formerly long, tousled hair was cut short in a utilitarian buzz cut. His body was different, too. As a dancer, he'd been all lean muscle and fluid grace, but the man standing before her seemed bigger, wider, taller than the friend she remembered.

She laughed self-consciously as she realized they were both simply staring at each other.

"Always knew how to make an entrance, didn't I?" she said.

"It's great to see you," he said. "I didn't realize you were in town. Where are you dancing? Or perhaps I should ask who's trying to steal the great Maddy Green away from the SDC?"

She opened her mouth to tell him her news, but nothing came out. Instead, a sob rose up from deep inside and she felt her face crumple.

"Hey," Max said. He moved closer, one hand reaching out to catch her elbow. "What's going on? Who's got you so upset?"

She pressed her face into the palms of her hands. She couldn't look at him when she said it. God, she could barely make herself say the words.

"They retired me. I had a knee reconstruction in July after I tore my anterior cruciate ligament. It's been coming along well, getting stronger, but the company's surgeon won't clear me to dance. So it's all over," she said, the words slipping between her fingers.

"Maddy. I'm so sorry," Max said.

She dropped her hands. "I didn't know what to do, where to go. And then I thought of you. And I caught the first plane to Paris. Didn't even bother to pack," she said. She tried to laugh at her own crazy impulsiveness, but the only sound that came out was an odd little hiccup.

Max's eyebrows arched upward and his gaze flicked to her dance bag, lying on the ground at her feet where she'd dropped it when he opened the door.

She understood his surprise. What kind of person took off around the world on the spur of the moment and lobbed on the doorstep of a man she hadn't seen in over eight years?

"Guess I wasn't really thinking straight," she said.

An icy breeze raced down the alley, rattling windows and cutting through the thin wool of her sweater. She shivered and Max shook his head.

"You're freezing." He tugged her through the doorway as he spoke, reaching to grab her bag at the same time.

"*Merde*. This thing is still as heavy as I remember," he said as he hefted the black suede bag.

The ghost of a smile curved her lips. Max used to give her a lot of grief about all the rubbish she hauled around. He always wondered how someone as small as she needed so much stuff.

One time he'd even tipped the entire contents onto the coffee table and made her justify every piece of detritus. They'd been laughing so hard by the time they got a third of the way through the pile that Maddy had begged him for mercy for fear her sides really would split.

"Girl's got to have her stuff," she said, the same response she'd given him all those years ago.

He smiled and kicked the door shut behind him.

"I was just opening a bottle of wine. That'll help warm you up," he said.

She glanced around as he led her across the large open space. Ancient beams supported the roof high overhead, and the walls were rough brick with the odd, haphazard patch of plaster smeared over them. A workbench lined one wall, filled with hand tools, and a row of sculptures sat side by side near a painted-over window.

She knew from the mass e-mail that Max had sent to his friends that he'd recently moved into a new apartment after the death of his father, but this was the last place she'd imagined him living. In the old days, he'd always been the one who complained the most about the moldy bathroom and crusty kitchen in their shared rentals. He'd even painted his bedroom himself because he couldn't stand the flaking, bright blue paint that had decorated his walls.

But maybe his appearance wasn't the only thing that had changed. Maybe the years had given him a different appreciation for what made a home.

"I was sorry to hear about your father," she said as he dumped her bag on a low modern leather couch. At least that conformed to her idea of the old Max's tastes—sleek, well-designed, high quality.

"Yeah. Thanks for the flowers, by the way. I can't remember if I sent a thank-you card or not," he said. "It's all a bit fuzzy, to be honest."

"You did."

They were both uncomfortable. She wondered if it was because she'd brought up his father, or because she'd miscalculated horribly in racing to him this way. She hadn't expected it to be awkward. She'd expected to walk through the door and feel the old connection with him. To feel safe and warm and protected.

Stupid. She could see that now. E-mails and Christmas cards and the occasional phone call were not enough to maintain the level of intimacy they'd once shared. She'd run halfway around the world chasing a phantom.

"Maybe I should come back tomorrow," she said, stopping in the space between his makeshift living zone and the counter, sink and oven in the back corner that constituted his kitchen. "You've probably got plans. I should have called before coming over. We can meet up whenever you're free."

Max put down the bottle of wine he'd been opening and walked over to stand in front of her. He reached out and rested his hands on her shoulders. The heavy, strange-but-familiar weight warmed her.

"Maddy. It's great to see you. Really. I wish it was for a happier reason, for your sake, but I'm honored you thought of me. Now, make yourself at home. I don't have a thing to do or a place to be. I'm all yours," he said.

More foolish tears filled her eyes. She blinked them away, then nodded. "Okay. All right."

He returned to the wine bottle, and she sat at one end of the couch. She was tired. Emotionally and physically. She felt as though she'd been holding her breath ever since Andrew had looked her in the eye and confirmed Dr. Hanson's pronouncement that her career was over.

"Here."

He slid a large wineglass into her hand. Red wine lapped close to the brim and she raised an eyebrow at him.

"Save me a trip back to the kitchen to get you another one," he said.

"I haven't been drunk in years," she said, staring down into the deep cherry liquid. "I guess if there was ever a time, this is it."

"Absolument," he said.

She drank a mouthful, then another.

"I was wondering what else was different about you," she said when she'd finished swallowing. "Apart from your hair and your face. It's your accent. It's much stronger now."

"That would come from speaking my native tongue for the past eight years," he said wryly. "These days, the only time I get to practice my English is when someone from the old days calls or visits."

"It's nice," she said. "The girls from the corps would love it. I remember they used to be all over you because of your accent."

"I think you're forgetting my stellar talent on stage and my legendary status as a lover," he said mock-seriously.

Her shoulders relaxed a notch as she recognized the familiar teasing light in his eyes. There was the old Max she knew and loved, the Max she'd craved when her world came crashing down around her.

"Right, sorry. I keep forgetting about that. What was that nickname you wanted us all to call you again?"

He snorted out a laugh and she watched, fascinated, as his face transformed.

He's been too serious for too long, she realized. *That's what's different about him, as well.*

She could only imagine what caring for his wheelchair-bound father must have been like. Terrifying, exhausting, frustrating and rewarding in equal measures, no doubt.

"The Magic Flute," he said. "I'd forgotten all about that. Never did catch on."

"We had our own names for you, don't worry," she said. She

toed off her shoes. As always, it was bliss to free her feet. If she could, she'd go barefoot all day.

"Yeah? You never told me that. What did you use to call me?"

He settled back on the couch. He filled the entire corner, his shoulders square and bulky with muscle.

"Not me, the corps. Wonder Butt was the most popular," she said. "Because of how you filled out your tights."

Another laugh from Max. The warm wine-glow in the pit of her stomach expanded. The more he laughed, the more the years slid away and the more she saw her old friend. Maybe it hadn't been so stupid coming here after all.

"Some of the girls called you Legs. Again, because of the way you filled out your tights."

"We'd better be getting to the Magic Flute part soon or I'm going to be crippled with size issues for weeks."

She felt her cheeks redden as she remembered the last nickname the other ballerinas had for Max. She shifted on the couch, not sure why she was suddenly self-conscious about a bit of silly trash talk. It had been a long time since she'd been coy or even vaguely self-conscious about anything sexual.

She cleared her throat.

"I believe they also used to call you Rex, too," she said.

He frowned, confused. She made a vague gesture with her hand. She couldn't believe he was forcing her to elaborate.

"You know. As in Tyrannosaurus Rex. Big and insatiable."

He threw back his head and roared with laughter. She found herself joining in.

"Maddy Green," he said when he'd finally stopped laughing. His light gray eyes were admiring as he looked at her. "It's damn good to see you. It's been too long."

A small silence fell as they both savored their wine.

"Do you want to talk about it?" he asked after a while. "Call people names, throw a tantrum? I'm happy to listen if you do."

She drew her legs up so that she was sitting cross-legged.

"I wasn't ready for it. I mean, they told me the surgery was a long shot, but I've always been a good healer. And the knee was getting better. If they'd just given me more time…"

She looked down and saw her left hand was clenched over her knee, while her right was strangling the glass.

"What did the doctor say?"

"A bunch of cautious gobbledygook about my body being tired and not being able to compensate anymore. I know my body better than any of them. I know what I'm capable of. I know I've got more in me. I can feel it here," she said, thumping a fist into her chest so vehemently that the bony thud of it echoed.

"Careful, there, tiger," he said.

She took a big, gulping sip.

"I still can't believe that Andrew took Hanson at face value like that. Like it was gospel."

"Hanson? I was wondering who treated you. He's supposed to be pretty good, right?"

She shrugged a shoulder dismissively. "Yes. The best, according to Andrew. Which is why they use him exclusively. But he's not the only doctor in the world. Remember Sasha? He was told he'd be crippled for life if he kept dancing, and he went on to score a place with the Joffrey Ballet. He's one of their lead soloists now."

He smiled. "Fantastic. Good for him. I've lost track of so many people, I've been out of it all for so long now. Is Peter still dancing? I tried to keep an eye out for him. Always thought he'd make it big."

"He got sick," she said quietly. "You know what he was like—never could say no."

Despite the well-known risk of AIDS, there were still plenty of beautiful, talented dancers who slept their way into an early grave. The travel, the physicality of the dance world, the camaraderie—passions always ran high, on and off the stage.

"What about Liza? I heard she'd gone to one of the European companies but then that was it."

Max and Liza had had a thing for a while, Maddy remembered. Was he thinking about making contact with her, now that he was free to make decisions for himself once again and Maddy had turned up on his doorstep, reminding him of the past?

"She's with the Nederlands Dans Theatre," she said. "I heard she'd gotten married, actually."

Max looked pleased rather than pissed. She decided he'd merely been curious about an old friend. For all she knew, he was involved with someone anyway. She'd seen no evidence that there was a woman in his life in his apartment, and he'd never mentioned a girlfriend in any of his e-mails, but that didn't mean a thing. He was a good-looking man. And there was that whole Rex thing. A man who enjoyed sex as much as Max apparently wouldn't go long without it.

She frowned. Since when had Max's sex life been of any concern to her? Their friendship had always been just that—a friendship. Warm, loving, caring and totally free of any and all sexual attraction on either side, despite the fact that they were both heterosexuals with healthy sex drives. Without ever actually having talked about it, they had chosen to sacrifice the transient buzz of physical interest for the more enduring bond of friendship. Which was why Max remained one of her most treasured friends—she hadn't screwed their relationship up by sleeping with him.

She lifted her glass to her lips and was surprised to find it was empty.

Maybe that was why she was wondering about things she didn't normally wonder about where Max was concerned—too much wine, mixed in with the unsettling realization that her old friend had changed while she'd been dancing her heart out around the world.

He pushed himself to his feet. "Let me fix that for you."

She watched him walk away, drawing her knees up to her chest and wrapping her arms around them. There was no hint of the lithe young dancer she'd once known in his sturdy man's walk. He still moved lightly, but his feet didn't automatically splay outward when he stopped in front of the counter, and there were no other indications that he'd once been one of the most promising, talented dancers she'd ever worked with.

Max had abandoned his career as a dancer to care for his father. Walked away just as his star was rising. At least she had had the chance to realize many of her dreams before Andrew and Dr. Hanson had written her off.

Her bleak thoughts must have been evident in her face when he returned because he shoved a plate of sliced, pâté-smeared baguette at her.

"Eat something, soak up that wine. I don't want you messy drunk too soon," he said.

"I'm off carbs," she said before she could think. "Need to drop weight."

How stupid was that? She didn't need to drop weight anymore. She could eat herself to the size of a house if she wanted to.

She looked at Max, desperately seeking some magic cure for the hollow feeling inside her.

"How did you do it?" she asked in a small voice. "How did you walk away? Didn't you miss it? Didn't you need it?"

He slid the plate onto the table. There was sympathy in his eyes, and old pain.

"I had lots of distractions. Worry over *Père,* practical things to sort out. I didn't have the time to think about it for a long while."

"And then?"

"It was hard. Nothing feels like dancing. Nothing."

She nodded, swallowing emotion. "It's my life. I've given it everything, every hour of every day."

"I know. It was one of the things I always admired about you. You were the most passionate dancer I knew."

Her jaw clenched.

"Sorry. I didn't mean to use past tense," he said.

God, he was so perceptive. Always had been.

"I can't believe it's over. It's too big, too much," she said.

A heavy silence fell. She could feel Max trying to find something to say, something that would make it all right. But there was nothing he or anyone could say or do. The decision had been made.

She shook her head and shoulders, deliberately shaking off the grim mood that had gripped her.

"Tell me about you. About your dad and…Charlotte, right? That's your sister's name, isn't it?"

They talked their way through the first bottle of wine and then the second. Maddy ate more than half of the bread and pâté and by ten was bleary-eyed with fatigue and alcohol.

"I need to go find a hotel," she said.

"Don't be ridiculous. You're staying here."

As soon as he said it, something inside her relaxed. She'd been hoping he would offer. She could still remember how she used to crawl into bed with him when it was cold and the heating wasn't up to the task of fending off the drafts from the many, many cracks and gaps in their house. The smell of Max all around her, the warmth of his body next to hers. He used to pull her close and she'd fall asleep with her head on his shoulder.

Just the thought of feeling that safe again made her chest ache.

"You can have my bed, I'll sack out on the couch," he said, standing to clear the dishes.

She stared up at him.

"I don't mind sharing with you. We used to sleep together all the time. Remember?" She hoped she didn't sound as desperate as she felt.

He hesitated a moment. "Sure. I'll try not to hog the quilt. It's been a while since I've shared with anyone."

She smiled up at him, relieved. "You know, I'm glad I came. It was a bit weird at first, but that was only because we hadn't seen each other for a while. And now it feels like the old days."

He looked away, his focus distant.

"The old days. Yeah."

"Do you mind if I have a shower first?" she asked.

"Of course not. I'll get you a towel."

He moved away, disappearing through a doorway to one side of the living area. Maddy began weaving her long hair into a braid to prevent it from getting wet.

She had no idea what tomorrow held. Even acknowledging that fact was a scary, scary thing for a dancer who had lived a life of strict self-discipline.

For a moment she got dizzy again and her heart began to pound. No rehearsal. No costume fittings. No classes. No gym or Pilates. What would she do with the time? God, what would she do with the *rest of her life?*

Max reappeared with a fluffy white towel and a fresh bar of soap.

"The bathroom's pretty primitive, but it gets the job done," he said.

The panic subsided as she looked into his clear gray eyes.

It would be all right. She was here with Max, and somehow she would find a way through this.

She stood and took the towel, then rested her hand on his forearm for a few seconds to feel the reassuring warmth of him.

Definitely she had done the right thing coming here, no matter how crazy it had seemed at first. Definitely.

MAX RAN A HAND ACROSS the bristle of his buzz cut as Maddy disappeared through the bathroom door.

Maddy Green. He couldn't quite believe that she was in his apartment after all these years.

The shock of seeing her on his doorstep continued to resonate within him. It was almost as though thinking of her today at his father's apartment had conjured her into his life.

She was still beautiful, with her long, rich brown hair and deep brown eyes. And being in the same room with her was still an experience in itself—her body vibrated with so much emotion and intensity, she was utterly compelling. It was one of the reasons she was such a joy to watch on stage—she had presence, star quality. She'd always drawn people to her.

He heard the shower come on and began collecting glasses and plates.

Her perfume hung in the air, something flowery and light. The same perfume she'd always worn.

Jesus. I still remember her perfume. How sappy is that?

A part of him was flattered that she'd thought of him in her hour of need. But he also wasn't sure how he felt about her barreling back into his life.

Once, she'd been the center of his world. He'd devoted half his twenties to loving her.

The wine bottles clinked together loudly as they hit the bottom of the recycle bin. Max wiped his hands on the thighs of his jeans.

His gut tightened as he thought of her news. Her career was over. Tough enough for someone like him to walk away from dancing. He'd only been in the early stages of his career. But Maddy had given her whole life to dance. She'd flown high— and the resulting fall was going to be long and painful.

He thought of her wounded look as she'd told him the doctor's verdict. Despite his ambivalence about seeing her again, he wished he could take away her pain. The old feelings still had that much of a hold on him. He didn't want to see her hurting.

He bounded up the stairs to the sleeping platform suspended above the kitchen zone. If she was staying in his bed, he needed to change the linen.

He was spreading a clean sheet across the mattress when she spoke from behind him.

"You didn't have to do that."

"Bachelor lifestyle." He turned, and something primitive thumped deep in the pit of his belly.

She wore one of his T-shirts. The hem hit her at midthigh and her hair was loose around her shoulders. He could see the soft outline of her nipples through the well-worn fabric. She'd always been small in the breast department, like most dancers, but she was nicely rounded and very perky. His gaze dropped to her bare, finely muscled thighs. Was she wearing any underwear?

Damn.

"I borrowed a T-shirt. Hope that was okay?"

He shifted his attention back to the sheet and concentrated on making the crispest hospital corners in the history of mankind.

"Sure."

"I've always wanted a loft," she said, wandering to the rail to look down over the rest of the apartment.

If he looked up, he knew he'd have a great view of her ass and the backs of her slim thighs. He kept his gaze fixed where it was.

Eight years had passed. How could he still want her so badly?

He glanced toward the stairs. It was one thing to want to comfort her, but it was another thing entirely to desire her. He'd been down that road before and he knew it went nowhere.

He unfolded the top sheet and flicked it hard to send it ballooning out over the bed.

You don't love her anymore. You stopped loving her years ago.

The thought sounded clear as a bell in his mind. Some of the tension left his shoulders. He was getting wound up about nothing. It was true—he'd gotten over Maddy long ago.

Stopped thinking about her, fantasizing, wondering. It had literally been years since he'd been a slave to his feelings for her.

Which was reassuring, but didn't quite explain the hard-on crowding his jeans.

She's a woman. A gorgeous, almost-naked woman. And you spent the better part of three years fantasizing about her. That kind of sexual attraction doesn't just die. But it doesn't mean anything except that you're horny, and she's hot.

He looked at Maddy.

She *was* a beautiful, sexy woman. That was undeniable. Probably any guy would feel something down south at the sight of her in his big T-shirt and precious little else.

Okay. Good. He'd rationalized his hard-on to death. Now he had to deal with the minor problem of their sleeping arrangements. The last thing he wanted was for Maddy to realize he was hot for her. She'd come to him seeking solace, not sex.

"You know, I think you'd be much more comfortable if I slept on the couch," he suggested casually. "I tend to toss and turn a lot. And you need to get over your jet lag."

She turned from studying his apartment, a frown on her face.

"I don't want to kick you out of your bed, Max. If you're worried about it, I'll sleep on the couch," she said.

"I'm not worried. I was just thinking of you."

A little too much, as it turns out.

"Well, if I get to choose, I'd rather sleep with you. I don't really want to be alone right now, you know?"

The lost look in her eyes sealed it for him.

"Fine. I'll just go brush my teeth," he said.

And try to find something to sleep in. Preferably something armor-plated.

By the time he'd brushed his teeth, discovered he had a choice of workout pants or boxer-briefs and opted—reluctantly—for the boxer-briefs since he could only imagine

Maddy's reaction if he rolled into bed wearing full sweats, ten minutes had passed. When he climbed to the sleeping platform, Maddy was curled up on one side of the bed, her eyes closed and her head pillowed on one hand.

She stirred as the mattress dipped under his weight.

"I thought you were never coming to bed."

"Had to put the dog out and check on the kids," he said.

She smiled faintly, her big eyes drowsy. Up close, he could see how fine and clear her skin was, as well as note the few endearing freckles that peppered her nose. She'd always hated them, calling them her bane and covering them every chance she got.

He smiled.

"What?" she asked.

"I'd forgotten about your bane."

She pulled a face.

"Trust you to notice them."

"They're cute."

"On a ten-year-old. Not on a prima ballerina. I bet Anna Pavlova didn't have freckles."

He saw the exact moment that she remembered, again, that she was no longer a prima ballerina. The light in her eyes dimmed and her full lips pressed together as though she was trying to contain something.

"Come here."

He held out an arm and she shifted across the mattress until she was lying against his side, his arm around her shoulders, her head on his chest.

If he kept concentrating on the lost, bewildered look in her eyes, he figured he had a fair to middling chance of pulling this off without embarrassing either of them. She needed him. That was enough to push all other thoughts into the background.

"It's going to be all right, Maddy," he said. "You'll see."

"I should have been ready for this. All ballet dancers have

to retire, I know that." Her words were a whisper. "Is it so wrong and greedy to want a little more? Another year? Two?"

Max tightened his embrace. He could feel how tense she was, could feel the grief and confusion in her.

"It'll be all right," he repeated, smoothing a circle on her back with the palm of his hand.

He felt the tension leave her body after a few minutes as the wine and jet lag and emotion caught up with her. He lay staring at the ceiling, listening to her breathing.

Knowing Maddy, she would probably be off home again tomorrow, her mad, impulsive trip having served the purpose of helping her express her grief and confusion. She had friends in Australia, a home. A life. She'd want to go back to the familiar as she tried to work out what happened next in the Maddy Green story.

She shifted in her sleep. As her perfume washed over him, a memory hit him. When they'd lived together, she'd left a scarf in his car after they'd gone to the movies one night. Rather than give it back to her, he'd hung on to it because it smelled of her perfume. A secret memento of Maddy.

Talk about besotted. He'd been so far gone it was a wonder the words hadn't appeared over his head and followed him around: *I am in love with Maddy Green.*

Another memory: the night he'd decided to tell Maddy how he felt. It had taken months to screw up his courage enough to risk their friendship. He'd arranged candles and red roses and bought a bottle of French champagne. The kitchen of their crappy rental had looked like a bordello by the time he'd finished decking it out—a kid's idea of a romantic scene, he recognized now. Then Maddy had come home, jumping out of her skin because she'd just been invited to join the Royal Ballet in London. He'd watched her unalloyed joy, untouched by regret for what she would be leaving behind. When she'd ducked off to call her mom, he'd quietly snuffed the candles and hidden the champagne in the back of the fridge and left his declaration unmade.

Thinking about it now, he could only thank God she'd been so preoccupied with her own news that she'd never thought to ask why she'd walked into the best little whorehouse in Sydney. She'd saved them both a painful and awkward conversation.

Maddy murmured in her sleep, her head moving on his shoulder restlessly. She rolled away from him, sprawling across half the bed.

He rolled the other way and resolutely closed his eyes. He had his first session with the life model he'd hired tomorrow. He needed to sleep, despite his circling thoughts and how aware he was of Maddy lying just a few feet away. He wasn't a kid, held to ransom by his body and his emotions. If the past eight years had taught him anything, it was to grab sleep when he could find it.

HE WOKE TO FIND HIMSELF curled into Maddy's back, her butt nestled into the cradle formed by his hips and thighs. One of his arms was wrapped around her torso.

He was painfully hard, his erection pressed against the roundness of her backside. So much for the protection of his boxer-briefs. His hand had somehow crept beneath her T-shirt to rest beneath the lower curve of her breasts. He could feel her ribs expand and contract as she breathed in and out.

She felt good. Small and sleek and feminine.

He knew he should back off, roll away before she woke and realized where she was and who he was and what was happening in his underwear.

He didn't move. He wanted to flex his hips and press himself against her so badly it hurt. His whole body tensed as he imagined sliding his hand a few vital inches and cupping her breast. He could almost feel the softness of it in his palm.

Thanks to the notorious lack of privacy in dancers' changing rooms, he'd seen Maddy in various states of undress over the years. She had small, pink nipples, and when she was cold they puckered into tight little raspberries.

He imagined plucking them, rolling them between his fingers. Pulling them into his mouth and tasting his fill of her.

His hard-on throbbed.

Man, oh man.

He closed his eyes. He had to back off. Now.

Maddy stirred, her body flexing in his embrace, her backside snuggling into his hips.

He'd never been so close to losing control in his life. His hand lifted from her torso. But instead of sliding it up and over her bare breasts, he twisted away from her warmth.

He slid to the side of the bed and sat up, scrubbing his face with his hands.

Talk about close. Too close.

His underwear bulging, he made his way downstairs. The cold water of the shower hit him like an electric shock, but it took care of business below stairs very effectively.

He eyed himself in the mirror as he shaved. He wasn't going to give himself a hard time for waking with an erection. It was pretty much an everyday occurrence, with or without a hot woman in his bed. He wasn't even going to give himself grief for horning onto Maddy while she slept. He was only human, after all.

But those few moments of temptation...

They were a whole other ball game. His jaw tensed as he imagined Maddy's reaction if she'd discovered him feeling her up. She'd come to him seeking comfort and understanding and he'd almost jumped her when she was at her most vulnerable.

Just as well she'd probably be going home tomorrow. He clearly couldn't be trusted where she was concerned.

Dressed in faded jeans and a long-sleeved T-shirt, he headed into the kitchen to make coffee. He worked as quietly as possible to fill the stovetop espresso maker. While he was waiting for it to brew, he cleared away some of the debris on the kitchen table. Which was when he saw the envelope icon flashing on his cell phone, indicating he had messages.

He clicked it open with his thumb, frowning when he saw it was a message from Gabriella, his life model.

pls call ASAP.

He dialed her number, a bad feeling in his gut. The message was time-stamped early this morning, and Gabriella was due in an hour. It didn't take a brain surgeon to realize something was up. As her phone rang and rang, he hoped the news wasn't terrible.

It had taken him over a month to find the body type he'd wanted to act as model for his latest project. The works he planned had been inspired by his years in dance, and he'd been excited when a mutual friend had put Gabriella in contact with him. She was a dancer—nowhere near Maddy's level, but she had the refined, defined muscles and flexibility he required.

He tried to anticipate the reason for the last-minute contact. She might be sick. Her car might have broken down. Or— disaster—she might have broken a leg or something else equally debilitating.

The phone clicked as someone answered.

"Max. I'm so glad you got my message," Gabriella said. "I was worried you wouldn't see it in time."

"Hi, Gabriella. What's up?"

"I'm so sorry, Max, but I won't be able to make it today. I got a job."

"Right. Congratulations." He tried to sound genuine. He knew that Gabriella had been looking for dancing work for some time now without much luck.

"I know this ruins your plans, but I had to take it," she said apologetically. "I hope you understand."

"Of course. We'll just reschedule. What's your timetable like? Is it weekend work?"

"Oh, I didn't explain very well, did I? The job's not here in Paris. It's a touring show, a kids thing. I'll be on the road for the next three months."

Shit. Might as well have broken a leg.

He leaned against the kitchen table and rubbed the bridge of his nose.

"Right," he said.

"I can still sit for you when I get back, if you're happy to wait," she offered tentatively.

"Sure. Give me a call when you're back in town."

He'd need to find someone before that, of course, but there was no need for Gabriella to feel needlessly bad. She had to make a living, and what he could pay her as a life model wouldn't come even close to what she'd earn as a full-time dancer.

"Okay. I'm really sorry for the short notice, Max."

"Don't worry about it. I'll work something out."

After wishing her best of luck with her new job, he ended the call.

He fought the urge to kick something. It had been a long time since he'd wanted something wholly for himself. Was it too much to ask that even the simplest of his desires—that his chosen model be available to sit for him at a convenient time—be answered?

"What's up?"

He turned to find Maddy halfway down the stairs. She was rumpled and sleep-creased and warm-looking. He made an effort to keep his eyes above the hemline of the T-shirt.

"Nothing. Just a work thing," he said.

"Of course. You're back in the workforce now. What are you doing?"

He stared at her. There were a handful of people who knew about his artistic ambitions. None of them were close friends or family. Still, he had to start owning his desires sooner or later.

"A bit of stonework. Mostly working with bronze. Mostly figure-based stuff," he said.

God, he felt like a pretentious wanker saying the words out loud.

She frowned. She had no idea what he was talking about, of course.

I'm trying to be an artist.

That's what he should have said.

Her baffled gaze slid over his shoulder to where his earlier works marched along the wall beside his workbench.

"Oh! Those are yours?" she asked, incredulous.

As well she might be.

Her eyes were wide as she walked over to inspect them.

"God, Max, I thought you'd brought them over from your dad's place or something and didn't know where to put them in your new loft," she said.

He stayed where he was, his whole body tense as she circled his most recent piece, a full-size bronze figure of a woman balanced on one leg, her other leg bent at the knee and held at a right angle from her body, her pointed foot hitting her supporting leg above the knee. Her arms were lifted high, joining in a graceful arch over her head.

He'd been happy with the emotion he'd been able to capture in the piece, but it still needed work.

"This is great! Wow. Max, this is amazing. I can't believe someone I know made something this beautiful."

Something—relief?—expanded in his chest and he let himself move closer.

Maddy ran a hand over the curve of the woman's waist and hip, her face lit with admiration.

"I can almost feel her moving. How did you do that?" she said. Then she snatched her hand away. "I'm so sorry! Is it okay if I touch it?"

Her expression was so contrite he had to laugh.

"It's bronze. It could probably survive a nuclear holocaust," he said.

She looked at him, shaking her head.

"I can't believe you didn't mention this last night, or in any of your e-mails, for that matter. I remember you used to sketch, but this is…I don't have the words. What a dark horse. How long have you been doing this?"

He shrugged. "I've just been dabbling, really. But I'm about to get started on a new series I've been planning."

"Was that what the call was about?"

"Yeah. Gabriella, my life model, pulled out at the last minute. I'm going to have to find someone else."

He sounded pissed. Probably because he was.

She'd moved on to inspect his smaller, earlier works. He shuffled from foot to foot, then shoved his hands into his back pockets. They weren't as good as they could be. He'd been learning his craft when he made them, honing his skills. He should have destroyed them. Or put them in storage somewhere.

Maddy's eyes were warm when she looked at him again.

"Max. I don't know what to say. These are really, really good."

He was embarrassed by how much her praise meant to him.

"Thanks."

She stroked the bronze figure again. "Losing this life model is a pretty big deal, yeah?"

"It's a setback. It took me a while to find her. The series is dance-based, and ordinary models aren't up to it."

"Dance-based." She looked at the bronze woman again. "Like this?"

"More dynamic. I want to capture that moment when dance

becomes more than just movement," he said. Then he stopped. Could he sound like any more of a tosser, crapping on about his work like some beret-wearing poseur?

She looked at him. There was a new light in her eye, as though she'd made an important decision.

"Use me," she said.

"Sorry?" He actually shook his head, convinced he hadn't heard right.

"You need a new life model, right? Someone to portray a dancer. Why not me?"

3

HE WAS GOING TO SAY NO. Maddy could tell by the way his eyes darkened and his jaw tensed.

She had no idea if she was the right model for what he wanted to do. But as soon as the idea popped into her head it had felt right. Especially given the realization she'd woken to this morning.

"Before you say no, hear me out," she said. "I decided something this morning. I'm not going to take this forced retirement lying down. I'm going to get a second opinion—hell, a fifth and sixth if I need it. I'm going to keep doing my rehab work and I'm going to find a way to dance." She said it like a challenge, daring him to disagree with her.

She'd given up too easily; the thought had been waiting for her, fully formed, when she opened her eyes and blinked at Max's ceiling half an hour ago. Dr. Hanson was one doctor, and she'd allowed his opinion to count for more than it should. She wasn't prepared to give up. Not yet. Not until she'd explored every avenue. Her future happiness depended on her efforts.

Only when Max nodded slowly did she release the breath she'd been holding. If he'd looked disbelieving—God, if he'd laughed—she wasn't sure what she would have done.

"I think that's a good idea," he said.

She smiled.

"Thank you. I needed to hear you say that. The thing is, most of the top dance medicine gurus are here in Paris. I couldn't be in a better place, even if I only came here because you were here. I'm going to call around today, try to get an appointment."

"That might take a while. Months, even."

"I know. I'm going to lean on some old colleagues to put in a word for me, see if I can't jump the waiting list."

"Stay here," he said. "It's no palace, but it's a roof."

She felt a rush of gratitude. The idea of staying with Max was infinitely preferable to twiddling her thumbs in a faceless hotel room for weeks while she gnawed her nails to the bone waiting for another specialist's pronouncement. But she couldn't mooch off him.

She said as much, and he made a rude noise.

"We're friends, Maddy. It's not mooching."

"Look, it's one thing to show up on your doorstep, drink your wine, eat your bread and crash in your bed for a night. But I can't foist myself on you for weeks at a time. Not unless you let me help you in return. That's why I offered to model for you. It would be a sort of barter—my body for your accommodation."

"You don't need to offer me a deal to stay here. You're welcome anytime."

"Thank you. But I can't live here and not offer anything in return. I know you well enough to know you won't accept money," she said. His instant frown was more than enough to prove her point on that score. "And, let's face it, my cooking skills aren't exactly great. Please let me do something for you in return for your helping me out."

"It's a sweet offer, but I don't think it's a good idea. If you really want to help out, I'm sure we can think of something else you can do."

She studied him, trying to understand his objection. He sounded so adamant, so immovable. Surely it would solve his problem as well as her own?

Or maybe he was just being polite. Maybe she was the last person he wanted to sketch.

"Is it because I don't have the right body type? It sounded like you were looking for a dancer's shape," she asked.

"It's not that." He rubbed a hand over the back of his neck, the picture of discomfort. "I don't think it'll work out, that's all."

He was over the conversation, she could tell, but she wanted to get to the bottom of this. She wanted to stay with him, but her pride wouldn't let her accept his hospitality without some kind of quid pro quo in place.

"Do you think I'll get fidgety, is that it? I promise I can stand still when I have to."

"It's not that."

She fiddled with the hem of the T-shirt, disappointed. "Okay. If that's the way you feel, I'll find a hotel this afternoon."

He looked annoyed. "Maddy. I said you could stay here, no strings. Don't be stubborn."

"I won't leech off you. I want to help. You're helping me, why can't I return the favor?"

"I would have thought that was pretty obvious. You've seen my stuff."

He gestured toward the row of statues. She glanced at them, then shook her head, baffled.

"Yeah. So?"

"My figures are all nudes, Maddy."

She blinked, then looked at the figures again.

Right. They were all naked forms. Huh.

"Well, that's no big deal, is it? It's not like you haven't seen me naked before. God, I think you know me better than my doctor after we did that season of *Wild Swans* together," she said.

Created by an avante-garde Australian choreographer, the ballet had been modern, intimate and daring. She and Max had worn thin body stockings and little else. By the end of the performance, they'd been so in tune with one another it had been hard to work out where his sweat finished and hers began.

"This is different," he said stubbornly.

She studied him closely and realized that color traced his cheekbones. He was embarrassed. Or self-conscious. Or maybe a bit of both.

"Max, you're blushing," she said. Mostly because she knew that nothing would get his back up faster. He might have changed, but not that much.

"No, I'm not."

"You're embarrassed at seeing me naked, aren't you?" She found the thought highly amusing. Had he really become so conservative?

"I was thinking about your comfort, not mine."

"Then there's nothing to worry about. Because I'm perfectly comfortable taking my clothes off in front of you. You're one of my oldest friends, for crying out loud. We used to live together, we've danced together. You even held my hair while I threw up after Peter's birthday party that time. We have no secrets, Max," she said.

He opened his mouth to object, but she waved a hand. "No. Not another word. You were planning to start this morning, yes?"

"Yes," he said grudgingly.

"Great. Then I'll have a shower and we'll get started."

She was still smiling when she closed the bathroom door on him.

Really, he was too cute. Worrying about her modesty. Totally wasted on her. Her body was the tool of her trade. She'd performed with dozens of male dancers throughout her career. Hands had caressed, gripped, slipped, pinched and God knows what else over the years. Standing naked in front of Max would be a piece of cake by comparison, and about as eventful for her as going to the supermarket was for other women.

It wasn't until she was standing in front of him, about to bare all that the first stab of self-consciousness hit.

She hadn't bothered dressing after her shower. She'd pulled on Max's oversize bathrobe, laced up the scuffed pair of ballet slippers she carried in her dance bag and stepped back into the main apartment.

He'd set up a stool for himself alongside a small table filled with charcoals, pencils and Conté crayons. A space heater had been turned on to ensure she wasn't too cold.

She took up position in front of him. Then she suddenly considered that maybe there *was* a difference between dancing intimately with someone while hundreds of people watched and standing completely naked in front of one man. Even if he was a friend.

Her fingers clenched around the tie on the bathrobe. Her stomach lurched with nerves.

She frowned, trying to work out why she was feeling…well, *shy* all of a sudden. She'd never been self-conscious about her body in her life. She knew she was in good shape, not an ounce of fat on her, her muscles lean and defined. Okay, she wasn't exactly a knockout in the rack department, but that had never bothered her before. Big breasts would only have gotten in the way when she danced, and that had always been the most important concern in her life.

But this morning she found herself wishing that instead of her half handfuls she had a little bit more action going on up top. Lord only knew how many women Max had slept with. She'd hate for him to look at her and find her lacking. Unfeminine, even.

She sneaked a glance at the bronze figure she'd admired earlier. Bronze Lady definitely had breasts. A good B cup, maybe even a C. Most of the time, Maddy didn't wear a bra at all. In fact, she had no idea what cup size she was these days. Which was something of a giveaway in and of itself.

Good grief, girl, get it together. Who cares if you have small breasts? Certainly not Max. You're a dancer, with a dancer's body. That's what he's looking for. Not tits and ass.

She forced her hands into action, unknotting the tie and almost throwing the robe open in her haste to get the moment of exposure over with.

She took a deep breath and made herself look up to make eye contact with Max. The sooner they normalized this situation, the better.

But he was busy with his supplies, selecting a pencil and sorting his charcoals into order.

Okay. Good. She had a few seconds to get her shit together without him watching her every move.

She slid the robe off her shoulders, letting it pool around her feet. The air was cool on her naked skin and she could feel her nipples tightening. She smoothed her hands down her hips and rolled her shoulders.

"Did you want my hair up or down?" she asked.

Max looked up at last. His gaze swept over her body. She couldn't read a single emotion on his face and she fought the instinct to cover herself with her hands.

"Up. I need the line of your neck and shoulders," he said. Then he returned his attention to his supplies.

She stared at him for a beat. Then she gathered the length of her hair and twisted it until it formed a loose knot on top of her head. She could feel her heart pounding in her chest, as though she was waiting in the wings, ready to run onstage and perform.

What had she expected him to say or do at first sight of her naked body? Break into applause? Go slack-jawed with admiration? Spout poetry?

She couldn't believe she was being so ridiculous. Juvenile, even.

When she focused on Max again, he was watching her, his expression still unreadable.

"How do you want me?" she asked.

He took a few seconds to answer.

"Let's start with first position, and move on from there."

She set her heels together and turned her feet out, joining her hands together in front of her and lifting them till they formed a gentle oval in front of her hips.

"Perfect," he said quietly.

She kept her eyes fixed on a point on the far wall. She could hear the soft rasp of pencil on paper as he began to sketch.

Five minutes passed, then ten. The room grew warmer. She let her gaze drift toward him. He was bent over his sketch pad, his hand moving quickly across the page as he split his attention between her and what he was creating. She wanted to talk, to ask him something to dispel the uncomfortable awareness she was feeling, but he was so inwardly focused she knew conversation wouldn't be welcome.

She forced herself to think of something else. Automatically her mind reverted to fretting over Andrew and her forced retirement from the company. There was no comfort to be found there, she knew. Instead, she started to make a mental list of her contacts in the various Paris-based ballets. She'd toured the country twice in her career and danced with several French soloists. Nadine, Jean-Pierre, Anna—they were just a few of the fellow dancers she could call on to ask for the favor of hooking her up with specialists. This afternoon, she would—

"Okay. Let's try some variations," Max said.

She blinked and let her body relax. "You're the boss."

"Third position this time," he said, eyeing her body assessingly. His regard was slow, steady. "*En pointe,* for as long as you can hold it."

"How long do you need?" she asked. She could hear the ego in her voice. He smiled.

"Not long," he said.

He started sketching, then stopped. "Can you look up for me?"

She lifted her chin. He frowned.

"Try angling your head a little more to the left."

She shifted. His frown deepened.

"It's not quite right…."

He stood and moved toward her. She stiffened, quelling the odd urge to retreat. Almost as though she was afraid of him, of his touch. Which was crazy. This was Max, after all. Her friend.

She could feel the heat from his body as he stood in front of her, studying the angle of her head. With her hands raised high above her, her weight supported on her toes, she was as tightly strung as a bow. And very exposed.

He reached out and nudged her chin up with his finger. A little higher. A little more to the left.

"That's good," he said.

His gaze swept the rest of her body and she felt a quiver of awareness deep in the pit of her belly. That odd instinct to retreat hit her again.

Then he was turning away, striding back to his sketch pad.

She took a deep breath, then another.

"You okay? Warm enough?" he asked as he took up his pencil.

She realized her breasts had puckered again, her nipples once more begging for attention. She fought a wave of self-consciousness.

"I'm fine," she said. "You just do your thing."

He took her at her word. She heard the scratch of pencil on paper and closed her eyes briefly. She felt rattled, off balance.

She forced her gaze to the back wall, concentrating on a crack in the plaster.

This is Max, she reminded herself. *Your friend. He held you while you slept last night. He's always been there for you.*

Slowly, by small degrees, she relaxed. There was no reason for her foolish awareness. Not with Max, of all people. He was like a brother to her. Always had been, always would be.

MAX TIGHTENED HIS GRIP on his pencil as he attempted to commit the curve of Maddy's hip to paper. His gaze kept sliding from the subtle arc of her waist down the flat planes of her belly to the curls at the juncture of her thighs. A neat little patch, waxed into submission, just enough curls there to hint at the secrets they concealed.

His hard-on throbbed. He still couldn't believe he'd let Maddy bulldoze him into this situation. But she'd been so determined to have her way. And he hadn't been strong enough to resist the temptation she'd offered. Back in the days when they'd lived together, he'd sketched her. Lying on the couch, asleep. Dancing, the expression on her face full of joy. Laughing, her eyes closed, her head thrown back.

But this was what he'd always wanted—Maddy gloriously, utterly naked, her body his to capture, if not to touch.

Heat flooded him as he remembered the temptation of standing close to her as he angled her head into position. He'd wanted to touch her so badly. To run his hands down her back to cup her pert, firm butt. To shape the small mounds of her breasts. To slide his fingers between her thighs and make her gasp with need for him.

Man.

He had to get his head together. He forced himself to concentrate on the paper in front of him, on the fine lines his pencil was shaping on the page. Slowly, Maddy's body emerged from the white. The taut readiness of her muscles. The discipline of her stance. The beauty of her features.

"Okay," he finally said.

She dropped down onto her flat feet.

"How's the knee?" he asked.

She frowned. "Fine. What next?"

She didn't like being reminded of her weakness.

"Arabesque *par terre*," he said.

Her frown deepened. "That's not very dynamic. I can hold *à la hauteur*," she said, referring to a pose where her back leg would be suspended in the air.

"I know. Show me an arabesque with your back leg on the ground first," he said.

She looked as though she was going to argue for a couple of beats. Then she gracefully moved into a sweeping arabesque, balancing on one leg while the other stretched out behind her, finally coming to a rest on the ground on her pointed toe. Her whole body arched into the pose, one hand extended behind her, the other in a straight line ahead. She looked as though she was about to take flight, the epitome of potential.

"Beautiful," he said involuntarily as he watched the play of muscles along her legs and torso.

Her breasts strained upward, and he could see her ribs expand and contract with every breath. Once again he was hopelessly torn between admiring her skill, wanting to capture her perfection on paper and needing to touch her so badly his groin was aching with it.

Start drawing, moron. It's going to be like this all morning. The sooner the session is over, the sooner you can have your sanity back.

His pencil held in a death grip, Max started to sketch.

An hour later, he'd captured a dozen poses and sustained a hard-on for longer than he'd thought was humanly possible. No matter what he told himself, or how many times he lost himself in the discipline of translating what his eye saw through his hand onto the page, his animal need for Maddy hummed constantly in the background.

By the time he put down his pencil and shut his sketch pad, he was literally shaking with desire.

He wanted to cross the space that separated them and get his hands on her so intensely that his mouth was dry and his belly contracted. It almost hurt to breathe, he was holding himself so tightly in check, in case his body sprang into action without his say-so.

"We're done?" Maddy said as she registered the slap of his sketchbook hitting the table.

"Yep."

Desperate to minimize the temptation, he strode forward and scooped up his bathrobe from where it lay pooled at her feet.

"Here," he said, holding the robe wide for her.

She turned her back and slid first one arm then the other into the sleeves. She reached up and tugged at the mass of hair knotted high on her head. Before he could pull away, it was tumbling down her back and over his hands. He stepped backward, but not before her scent surrounded him.

"I might grab a shower," he said abruptly.

They'd only been working for three hours and he'd hardly broken a sweat, but he had to get away from her. And he had to do something about the tent pole in his jeans before she saw that her good friend was packing wood.

Embarrassing? *Oui.* Big-time.

"Okay," she said. "I noticed a *boulangerie* on the corner yesterday. I could go get us some bread for lunch, maybe some quiche," she said.

"Great idea," he said, already heading for the bathroom. Her plan had the added advantage of getting her out of his apartment for five minutes. Long enough for him to get a grip on himself. He hoped.

The bathroom door safely closed behind him, Max shed his clothes and stared down at his straining boner. His body had a mind of its own where Maddy was concerned. No matter what he knew to be true—that it was never going to happen with her—his body had other ideas.

He twisted on the cold tap. Then he gritted his teeth and stepped beneath the spray.

Chill water hit him like a slap. He closed his eyes, willing his body into submission.

After a good minute, he glanced down at his resilient, determined hard-on, still standing proudly. Whoever heard of an erection so stubborn, so deeply committed to its cause that it could withstand the brutal effects of a cold shower?

His skin pebbled with gooseflesh, he finally gave up and twisted on the hot tap. There was more than one way to skin a cat, after all. Reaching for the soap, he lathered his palms until they were slippery and reached for his erection.

A few minutes, fast and furious, ought to take care of business—and hopefully keep his body under control for the rest of the day.

He closed his eyes and angled his face away from the spray. Hot water hit his chest and ran down his body in rivulets as he stroked his shaft.

Sensation washed through him and images filled his mind. The soft outline of Maddy's breasts against his T-shirt. The curve of her butt pressed against his hard-on this morning. The dark, mysterious shadow between her thighs as she posed for him. The puckered pinkness of her nipples, tight from the cold.

He tried to force his thoughts away from Maddy, but for the life of him he couldn't summon up an image of Marie-Helene or Jordan. Could barely remember their faces, let alone their bodies. He wanted Maddy. And, so help him, in the safe confines of the shower and his mind, he was going to have her.

He gave himself up to the fantasy. A dozen scenarios flitted across his imagination, but he settled on the one that best suited the moment.

He imagined Maddy entering the bathroom, wearing nothing but his robe. He could almost see her standing there, steam rising around her as she let the robe slide to the floor.

He groaned in the back of his throat as he imagined himself touching her at last, pulling her close, kissing her, plunging his tongue inside her mouth, his hands racing over her body.

Squeezing her breasts, teasing her nipples. Nudging a knee between her thighs. Sliding a hand into that tempting thatch of curls, then into her slick folds.

She'd be wet for him. So wet and ready that when he slicked a finger over her she'd twist and moan. He'd bend her over his arm and pull a nipple into his mouth, sucking and biting her. He'd keep stroking between her thighs, slicking over and over her until she begged him to give her what she needed.

Max's fist worked up and down his shaft, his eyes tightly closed as he lost himself in the rising tide of his own desire.

He'd push Maddy against the tiles, cup her butt in his hands and lift her till he could slide inside her. She'd be so tight and wet. She'd grip him with her inner muscles and he'd start to pound into her. Deep, hard, relentless. His hardness to her wet softness. Her need meeting his.

He frowned as desire built within him and guilt warred with need. He knew he shouldn't be eroticizing Maddy this way, that it would only make things more difficult, not less. But he was so close. Just this once, he promised himself. Just this once he'd indulge himself where Maddy was concerned.

His hand a blur, Max pushed himself toward the edge.

MADDY GRABBED HER PURSE and slung the strap over her shoulder. The bakery was just a few steps away on the corner, but she pulled on Max's coat for the short walk. When she'd arrived last night, she'd had a taste of how bitterly cold a Parisian winter could be, and she didn't need to learn the same lesson twice. She needed to shop for a coat of her own and a bunch of other stuff now that she'd decided to stay. The few tops and changes of underwear she'd thrown into her dance bag were barely good for a couple of days.

She was on her way out the door when the phone rang. She turned, eyeing it uncertainly for a beat, waiting for an unseen answering machine to pick it up. But the phone rang and rang. Finally she returned to the living space and picked up the receiver. If Max objected to her answering his phone, she'd find out soon enough.

"Max's apartment," she said.

There was a short, surprised silence before a woman spoke in accented English. "Is Max there? I need to speak to him."

"Um, he's in the shower. I can pass on a message," Maddy suggested. She hoped like hell this wasn't a girlfriend who would get the wrong idea about her and Max from the fact that she was in his apartment answering his phone.

"No. I need to speak to him now. Tell him it's his sister. Tell him it's about Eloise."

There was an urgency in Charlotte's voice that was undeniable.

"Give me a second, I'll get him for you."

Phone in hand, Maddy crossed to the bathroom door and tapped lightly.

"Max. It's your sister. It sounds urgent," she said through the door.

Nothing. She tapped on the door again.

"Max, I think your sister really needs you," she said more loudly this time.

Still nothing. She could hear the splash of water on the other side of the door. She knew from experience how noisy Max's stall could be with water pounding on the tiles and the plastic shower curtain.

She eased the door open, very aware of Charlotte waiting. Maddy hoped she wasn't about to embarrass herself and Max by barging in on him. There was a shower curtain, after all. And since the shower was still going, there was no chance she'd catch Max drying off. So this wasn't a total invasion of privacy.

She felt faintly stupid even worrying about catching him naked, given she'd just spent the past three hours posing in the buff for him. There was nothing he had that she hadn't seen before, after all.

"Max," she said as the door swung open.

The rest of what she'd been going to say got stuck somewhere between her lungs and her mouth as she saw that the shower curtain wasn't fully pulled across and that she had a perfect view of Max standing under the water, erection in hand, a look of pleasurable pain on his face as he stroked himself toward fulfillment.

He was totally oblivious to everything except the matter in hand and she literally didn't know what to do. Breathe. Retreat. Say something. Die on the spot.

She couldn't take her eyes off him. Golden skin, covered in fine dark hair. A muscular body, bunched and flexed slightly forward as he neared his climax. Strong thighs. And a powerful-looking erection that jutted arrogantly from his body.

He groaned, a low sound that snapped her into focus. Heat rushed up her body, sending prickling tendrils beneath her armpits and the back of her neck before filling her face with warmth. Eyes glued to Max, she took a step backward, her shaking hand reaching for the door handle as she pulled it shut behind her.

Oh, boy.

Her knees were weak. She felt hot, as though she'd been rehearsing for hours. She fanned herself, then suddenly remembered the phone call.

The receiver was still in her left hand. She lifted it to her face.

"He won't be a minute." Her voice came out as a croak. "He's just getting out of the shower."

Then she counted to ten before knocking very, very loudly on the bathroom door. Opening it a crack, she hollered through the gap.

"Max, your sister is on the phone. It sounds important," she said.

She left the phone on the kitchen table where he would be sure to find it and hightailed it toward the door.

Once she was outside she walked up the street and around the corner before she felt safe enough to stop.

She was shell-shocked. There was no other word for it. She'd caught Max touching himself, on the brink of having an orgasm, and she was blown away.

She leaned against the wall of a building and closed her eyes. Instantly she was in the bathroom again with Max naked and aroused, his hand sweeping up and down his shaft, his head thrown back, his whole body tense with anticipation.

God, he'd looked amazing. So...masculine. She huffed out a small, humorless laugh at how woefully inadequate her vocabulary was. *Masculine* didn't even come close to describing how vital and overwhelmingly male he'd looked with his legs braced apart, his back against the wall, all that hardness in his hand.

No wonder they called him Rex.

The thought popped into her mind before she could censor it.

"Oh, God," she said, pressing her hands against her burning face.

She should not be thinking about his generous schlong. Definitely she shouldn't. It was wrong, wrong, wrong. He was her friend, her lovely, platonic friend who had danced with her, lived with her, laughed with her, cried with her.

And now she knew with absolute clarity how he looked naked. And not just *undressed* naked, either. She knew how he looked fully aroused, ready-to-go, big-and-proud naked. And she didn't know what to do with her new knowledge.

"Max is my friend," she said out loud.

An old man braving the cold to walk his dog gave her a curious glance as he passed by.

Great. She was a voyeur *and* a crazy, talking-to-herself-in-the-street person.

She pushed her frozen hands into her coat pockets and turned toward the *boulangerie*. Her French was rusty, but she managed to greet the woman behind the counter and buy half a dozen croissants and a baguette. The baguette was fresh from the oven and the paper bag it was wrapped in grew warm in her hand as she walked the short distance to Max's front door.

She had no idea what to say to him. Or how she would look at him without breaking into a sweat.

She should have knocked louder. And closed her eyes or looked the other way when she opened the door. Better yet, she should have let his answering machine take the call.

She was going to have to simply pretend it had never happened. There was no other alternative. She certainly wasn't about to tell Max what she'd seen—God forbid.

She knocked, then swallowed a lump of acute discomfort as she heard footsteps moving toward the door. Just like yesterday, except this time she wasn't imagining her old dancing buddy on the other side. No. Now she was imagining a naked, rampant man with a huge—

"Hey. I was wondering what was taking you so long," Max said as the door swung open.

He was fully dressed. Thank heaven for small mercies.

"There was a queue," she fibbed.

"I have to go to my sister's. She's had some problems with her latest babysitter. I'm going to go hold her hand for a while," he said. "I might be a while."

"Okay."

For some reason, she was having a lot of trouble keeping her attention fixed on Max's face. Her gaze kept wanting to slide down his chest to his crotch. Like a criminal returning to the scene of the crime.

"I've left a spare key for you on the kitchen table. Feel free to use the phone, the Internet, whatever. And don't wait for me if it gets to dinnertime and I'm not back."

"Sure. Don't worry about me. Your sister sounded really worried."

He sighed. "Yeah. She gets worked up sometimes. Her husband travels a lot and she struggles with the kids on her own. I couldn't help out as much as I wanted to when *Père* was still alive, but now it's better."

He was worried, distracted. She bet he was a great brother, despite his own assessment. She knew how great he'd been with her. No doubt he moved mountains for his sister. Which was why it was wrong, twisted, just plain freaky that she kept getting flashbacks to the shower scene as she looked at him. One second Max was standing decently clothed in front of her, her old friend looking platonically handsome and solid and reliable in faded denim and a chunky-knit sweater, and the next he was naked, gorgeous, hard as a rock and about to lose it.

"You'd better get going," she said.

Like, right now. Before my head explodes from all the illicit images bouncing around inside it.

She stepped aside to clear the way to the door.

"I've got my cell phone with me. Call if you need anything," he said.

He gave her a friendly pat on the shoulder as he passed. She found herself staring at his butt as he walked away, mesmerized by the perfection of his rounded, hard ass. A dancer's ass, even though he'd long since retired. Wonder Butt, indeed.

She registered what she was doing and made a frustrated noise in the back of her throat as she shut the door behind him.

One look. Ten seconds, maximum, and she felt as though nothing would ever be the same again. Which was crazy. She and Max had known each other for more than ten years. One moment of full exposure couldn't shift their friendship so profoundly.

Could it?

"No," she said out loud, just to hear the certainty in her own voice.

Barely twenty minutes had passed since she walked into the bathroom. Of course she was feeling antsy and uncomfortable still. The image of Max all hot and bothered was etched large in her memory. But it would fade. Soon, it would even be funny.

She frowned.

Okay, maybe not *soon*. But definitely what she had seen would be amusing one day, rather than disturbing and unsettling in ways that she simply wasn't prepared to examine.

She spent the rest of the day chasing up contact numbers for her dancing colleagues and making phone calls. Jean-Pierre and Anna both offered to contact their specialist, Dr. Rambeau. Apparently he was young but innovative and growing in reputation. She couldn't get through to Nadine and left a message, crossing her fingers that she wasn't out of town performing.

By midafternoon, Max still wasn't home. Maddy did some Pilates and worked her way through a series of stretches and strength-building exercises. Darkness came early, and at six she rummaged through the few groceries on Max's shelves and wound up having more pâté spread on bread for dinner. She switched on the TV afterward, but her French wasn't strong enough to make much sense of anything. By nine she was tucked in Max's bed, one ear cocked for the front door as she waited for him to come home.

She was wearing his T-shirt again, and his aftershave clung to the sheets. She shifted restlessly, feeling tense and edgy. No matter how hard she tried to distract herself, she kept thinking about what she'd seen.

She punched her pillow then rolled onto her back and glared at the ceiling. Why was seeing Max in such a revealing way so confronting for her? Yes, she'd walked in on an intensely personal, private moment, and if Max had seen her, they both would have been embarrassed. But he hadn't. So there was no reason for her to feel so…itchy and scratchy. No reason at all.

She swore and rolled onto her stomach, burying her face in the pillow.

The truth was, a long time ago she'd made a decision to ignore any attraction she felt for Max in order to keep him as a friend. He'd been startlingly attractive as a young man, and like a lot of the women in the Danceworks company, she'd taken one look at him and felt the tug of desire.

But at nineteen years old, Maddy had already learned the hard way that men and ballet didn't mix. No matter how much any man admired her skill, no matter how great the sex was, jealousy and resentment always drove a wedge between her and her lovers.

She'd been burning from the latest breakup with the most recent of her boyfriends when Max joined Danceworks, and as much as she was attracted to him, she'd seen the writing on the wall without even squinting. A few months of hot sex, fun and laughs. Then the demands would start. The sulking. The fights. The cold silences. Finally, the angry betrayal with another woman. Or—worse—the angry ultimatum. She'd been there, done that, and a few conversations with Max were enough to make her not want to go to the same ugly, sad place with him. He'd been so funny and smart and generous. She'd felt instantly comfortable with him, and she'd made a conscious decision not to let sex become a thing between them. He'd become her first and best male friend.

And now she'd caught a glimpse of the virile, sexual man behind her dear friend and she was afraid that she wouldn't be able to forget it.

Because the real, stark, unadorned truth was that seeing Max in such a blatantly sexual situation had been a huge turn-on. The unrestrained need in him, the intensity of his expression, the hard strength of his body—even now she felt a rush of damp heat between her thighs.

For the first time in over ten years of friendship, she was looking and thinking of Max as a potential lover and not as her friend.

And that scared the hell out of her.

4

IT WAS LATE when Max eased the front door open. He paused on the threshold, listening. The apartment was silent. Maddy had gone to bed.

Good.

He carried the foldaway camp bed his sister had loaned him inside and propped it against the wall. She'd raised an eyebrow when he'd asked if he could borrow it. His explanation that he had an old friend staying for a few days hadn't gone far toward satisfying her curiosity. She'd already been suspicious of his continuing presence in her apartment.

The crisis she'd called him over—a problem with the latest babysitter the agency had sent—had been resolved in the first hour. Charlotte had really only wanted a stand-in for her absent husband, a shoulder to cry on while she expressed her fury and disappointment that her little girl had once more been let down and misunderstood.

Her gratitude had slowly turned to inquisitiveness as the hours wore on and he'd stayed to help bathe Marcel and Eloise then cook dinner. By the time he'd settled beside her on the couch after dessert she'd been looking at him out of the corners of her eyes, clearly wondering why he was still hanging around.

He'd been avoiding going home, and they'd both known it. As soon as he mentioned the bed and the fact he had an old dancing friend staying over, he'd seen the cogs begin to turn in his sister's mind. Which was why he'd made his escape and finally come home. He wasn't up for twenty questions regarding his friendship with Maddy. Not that there was a lot to discuss; he just preferred not to have his sister jumping to conclusions.

He eased off his shoes and crossed to the stairs. He could make out the pale oval of Maddy's face on the pillow as he moved toward the chest where he kept his spare linen and blankets. He found a sheet by feel, then what he hoped was a pillowcase.

"Is everything okay at your sister's?"

Light washed over the bed as Maddy flicked on the lamp and propped herself up on one elbow.

"She was fine once she calmed down. Just a problem with an inexperienced babysitter. Sorry, I didn't mean to wake you."

"I wasn't really asleep, anyway." She frowned when she registered the linen in his arms. "Max, tell me you weren't about to sneak down to sleep on the couch," she said.

"I borrowed a camp bed from Charlotte. If you're going to stay for a while, I figured you might prefer a bit of privacy."

There was a moment of silence. He felt about as transparent as a teenager. It didn't help that the mere sight of her in his bed springboarded him into about a million different sexual fantasies.

She threw back the covers.

"I told you, I'm not stealing your bed. If anyone is sleeping on the camp bed, it's me," she said.

She stood and crossed the space between them, pulling the folded sheet from his hands.

"Wait a minute," he said, trying to grab it back.

She stepped away and shook her head. "No. You're already doing me the hugest favor, letting me crash here. Plus, I'm about half your size. There's no way you'll be more comfortable on a camp bed than me."

He started to protest again, but she held up a hand.

"Have you got a spare quilt?"

She turned and grabbed her pillow from his bed, tucking it under her arm. She looked immovable and determined. He yanked a thick duvet from the chest.

"Maddy, this is crazy. I've slept on the camp bed a million times, it's no big deal. We kept it for when *Père* was bad and needed constant care in his room."

"Not listening," she said as she started down the stairs.

He had no choice but to follow her. She was wearing his T-shirt again, and he was acutely aware of her bare legs beneath it and the way her pert backside swayed from side to side with each step.

"Help me set this thing up," she said, eyeing the bed frame.

"Maddy. This isn't what I brought it home for," he said.

"Stop being so damn noble." The bed frame protested with a rusty groan as she unfolded it flat. "I've slept in far worse places, believe me."

She tugged the duvet from his arms.

"Go to bed. You've spent the whole day thinking about everyone else. Get some sleep."

He stared at her. If only she knew that from the moment she'd arrived on his doorstep she'd dominated his thoughts, pushing almost everything and everyone else aside.

The realization made him turn away. Maddy was a friend in need. That was all. His days of obsessing over her were in the past.

"Fine, you win. I'll see you in the morning," he said over his shoulder.

"Night, Max."

Upstairs, he stripped to his boxer-briefs and slid into bed. The sheets were still warm from her body. He lay on his side, staring at the wall. He could hear her moving around downstairs, making the bed up. Then there was nothing but silence.

If he hadn't brought the bed home, she'd be beside him right now, the sound of her breathing soft in the darkness.

He rolled onto his belly and fisted his hand beneath the pillow.

Getting the camp bed had absolutely been the smart thing to do. He just wished like hell he didn't regret doing it quite so much.

FORGET ABOUT what you saw. Go out there, take your clothes off, start working. Max is waiting for you.

Maddy reached for the bathroom door handle for the third time that morning, and for the third time she hesitated.

She'd spoken to Max yesterday. Argued over the camp bed last night, in fact. So it wasn't as though this was their first meeting post-shower scene. There was absolutely no reason for her to be loitering in the bathroom. Hadn't she decided this wasn't going to be an issue between them, that she was going to push the memory of what she'd seen into the very darkest corner of her mind and ignore it?

"Idiot."

She pushed the door open and marched into the apartment. Her stomach dipped as she stopped in front of Max. He was sitting on his stool opening a new box of charcoals, his head bent over the task. She watched the muscles work in his forearms, the way his deft fingers teased the packaging open. Instantly she flashed to an image from yesterday: Max's arms rigid with tension, his biceps flexing as his fist slid up and down his erection.

He glanced up, a frown on his face. Almost as though he'd somehow guessed what she'd been thinking.

"I forgot to ask. How did you get on with the specialists yesterday?"

She blinked stupidly at how normal the question was. While she agonized over the illicit glimpse she'd inadvertently gotten into his sex life, it was business-as-usual for Max. He didn't know what she'd seen. He never would.

"Really well. I spoke to Anna yesterday and she texted me

first thing this morning. She got me an appointment next week with her specialist, Dr. Rambeau."

"That's great news."

"He hasn't got a huge reputation, but both Anna and Jean-Pierre swear by him. Now I just have to contact Dr. Hanson and get my records sent over." Frankly, she'd rather chew glass but it was something that had to be done.

"Not looking forward to it?" His gray eyes were sympathetic.

"Asking for a second opinion is a slap in the face, no matter how you look at it. He's not going to be gracious about it," she said. And, rational or not, she was angry with Dr. Hanson. Both he and Andrew had given up on her before she'd had a chance to prove herself. The last thing she wanted was talk to either one of them.

"Want me to do it for you?"

"Yeah. But I'm not going to let you. You know, Monsieur Laurent, I'm beginning to think you have a bit of a Sir Galahad complex. You're always primed to ride to my rescue at the drop of a hat."

He made a dismissive noise.

"What do you call trying to sleep on the camp bed last night?"

He looked caught out.

"Exactly. You're too gallant for your own good."

"Humph."

"What?"

"My sister said something similar the other day."

"Well, then, it must be true."

He smiled, and she smiled back, and for a long moment they enjoyed the camaraderie.

See? This is normal. Just like old times, B.S.S. Before Shower Scene.

Then he looked at his watch.

"Guess we'd better get started, huh?" she said.

That quickly, she was nervous again.

"Guess so. Unless you need to do something else today?"

"No. Nothing else." Unfortunately.

She reached for the sash on the robe. This was her way of repaying Max for his hospitality. It was the least she could do for him.

She let the robe slide down her arms.

Like yesterday, he was busy organizing his pencils when she looked at him. She turned her feet out and pulled in her belly and squared her shoulders.

"Okay, I'm ready when you are," she said.

He barely glanced up. It struck her again how commonplace this must be for him. She was simply another model, another body. Which made it even more stupid and pointless to feel so self-conscious and uncertain.

"Let's start with fourth position, *en pointe*," he said.

She moved smoothly into the pose, concentrating fiercely on achieving perfect form and posture. Anything to stop herself from thinking about the fact that she was standing naked in front of Max, and that yesterday he'd been so hard and—

Enough!

She gritted her teeth and arched her back a little more. He began to sketch. She kept her mind busy reviewing the choreography for the production of *Giselle* she'd been rehearsing before Dr. Hanson ended her career. After ten minutes, Max asked for a second pose, then a third, each of which she held for close to fifteen minutes as he worked. Nearly an hour later, he paused to flick through his sketch pad. She stretched out her calf muscles and surreptitiously massaged her bad knee.

"Do you feel up to something more dynamic?" he asked.

His gaze was on her knee. He'd caught her rubbing it. She turned her feet out and stood tall.

"Whatever you've got."

"I don't want to aggravate your injury."

"You won't. It's healing. Work is good for it," she said. "I have to start building my strength up again."

He looked doubtful. Self-consciousness forgotten, she rose up *en pointe* and began a series of battements, her feet flashing as she flicked one pointed foot in front of the other in a rapid, beating movement, her arms held in a graceful curve at midchest height.

"Okay, okay. Point taken," he said, shaking his head.

"What were you thinking of?"

"Do you remember the season of *La Sylphide* we did right before I left the company? There was that series of *fouetté rond de jambe tournants* toward the end of the last act."

She tried to recall the choreography he was referring to. It had been a long time ago and there had been many, many sequences since.

Max stood and took up position, rising up onto his toes in his bare feet. Despite the fact that it must have been years since he danced professionally, his form was perfect as he began to spin on his left foot, his right leg raised and bent at the knee as he demonstrated a *fouetté*. His right leg whipped around his body again and again as he spun, powering his turns, while his arms were held extended at shoulder height.

"Yes! I remember now," she said. The sequence spilled into her mind in an unbroken chain. The *grand jeté*, followed by the increasingly frantic *fouettés*, then the despairing collapse and surrender at the end.

Max stopped, barely breathing hard from the exertion.

"Still got the old moves, Max," she said admiringly.

He'd been such a wonderful dancer. Watching him was like seeing a ghost from the past.

A shadow passed over his face. Yearning, regret, disappointment—she saw it all in his eyes for a few unguarded seconds before he picked up his sketch pad.

"A few more rotations and I probably would have spun into a wall or torn a muscle," he said dismissively.

She took a step toward him.

"Do you think you can hold the end position for me?" he asked without looking up.

She stilled. He didn't want to talk about it or acknowledge his reaction. For a long beat she considered how she would feel if their positions were reversed. Then she pivoted on her heel and walked to the farthest corner of his work space.

Some things were too painful and private to talk about.

When she turned to face him, he was once more armed with his charcoals.

I don't ever want to know what it feels like to not have dance in my life.

The thought came from her gut. Rationally, she knew she had to retire someday. No dancer could perform forever. But she wasn't ready to hang up her slippers yet. Not even close. The thought of losing the most important, fulfilling thing in her life was unthinkable. Unbearable.

"Do you have enough space?"

"Yes."

She pulled her focus into her body. She reviewed the choreography in her mind, then found her starting point. With an explosion of power she sprang into a *grand jeté*. Her muscles stretched and her body soared as she leaped across the space. Everything receded into the background. She landed and rotated fluidly into the first *fouetté*. Her support leg *en pointe,* she spun, her working leg whipping the turn to greater speed with each rotation.

As her speed increased, her moves become more desperate, more frantic. She allowed her spin to waver, let her arms drag her off balance. Finally, she fell out of the spin, collapsing onto the ground in an abandoned-yet-controlled sprawl, one leg bent beneath her, the other stretched forward, her body draped over it in a posture of absolute despair and defeat.

There was a moment of silence. She could hear her own breathing, feel her chest heaving against her extended leg.

"Beautiful, Maddy. Beautiful."

She heard him begin to draw. She kept her body alert despite the temptation to relax into the stretch. She knew without asking that Max wanted the dynamic tension of the position and the emotion of the dance, not simple anatomy.

After five minutes, her body began to stiffen. She concentrated on each protesting muscle in turn, tensing and releasing them without changing posture. After ten minutes, she heard the scrape of Max's stool on the floor.

"That was great. Absolutely what I was looking for," he said as he approached.

She allowed herself to sit upright at last. He extended a hand to help her to her feet. She started to rise, but the leg that had been bent beneath her buckled, refusing to hold her weight. She stumbled, but his arms were around her before she could fall, one big hand splaying beneath her rib cage, his fingers grazing the lower curve of her right breast, the other grabbing her hip. Instinctively she reached for him, too, one hand finding his shoulder, the other his back.

For a shocking moment she was pressed against him, breast to chest, hip to groin.

She froze.

The soft fabric of his T-shirt brushed against her breasts. She inhaled pure Max—soap and sandalwood. She could see each individual hair of his morning stubble, the whiskers black against his olive skin, and feel his warm breath on her cheek.

Her heart began to pound against her rib cage. If he moved his hand, he would be cupping her breast in his palm.

The thought made her tremble with sudden, hungry need. Her nipples tightened in anticipation.

"You okay now?"

She could feel his deep voice vibrating through her body.

"Yes," she said, even though it was a big fat lie.

His grip slackened and he stepped away from her.

The loss of his heat and hardness was a shock. She blinked and tried to pull herself together. She was afraid to look at him, afraid he would see only too readily the thoughts that had been racing through her mind. She ducked to collect her robe, painfully aware of her aroused nipples. Only when she'd tied the sash did she dare look at him again.

He was studying the drawing he'd completed, an expression of concentration on his face. He seemed utterly unaware of the fact that he'd just held her naked body pressed against him and that she was vibrating with the aftershock of the contact.

"I think we're done for the day," he said. "That last pose was great, Maddy. Thanks." He looked up, his face unreadable. "Sometimes I forget what it's like when you dance."

She stared at him for a long moment. How was it possible that she'd felt so much when he held her while he was completely unaffected?

You don't want him to be affected. He's your friend. Sex is the best way to destroy that. Remember how every relationship you've ever had has ended?

She tightened the sash on the robe again. For the second time in as many days, Max had reduced her to incoherent jelly. It confused the hell out of her, as well as being damned embarrassing. She could only imagine how he'd respond if he knew what was going on in her head. Since when did old friends suddenly want to jump each other?

She crossed to the camp bed and scooped up her clothes. In the bathroom, she dressed quickly, ignoring the sensitivity of her skin and the telltale heat between her thighs. She stared at her reflection in the bathroom mirror.

"What are you doing?" she asked herself, her voice low and serious.

She'd come to Max seeking sanctuary, not sex. She was on the verge of making a mistake she knew she would regret for the rest of her life.

He was at the kitchen table working on one of his sketches when she emerged.

"I'm going out," she said, hovering awkwardly at a distance. "I need to buy some things. A coat, another pair of shoes." *And get away from you for a few hours.*

"Sure. I should be around but take the spare key. I want to do some more work on these sketches."

"I'll bring something back for dinner. Maybe some chicken fillets," she said vaguely.

He surprised her by laughing.

"What's so funny about chicken fillets?"

"Have you had cooking lessons or bought a cookbook since we last lived together?" He was grinning at her, highly amused.

"I signed up for some classes, but I never got there," she admitted.

"So what were you planning on doing with the chicken?"

"Something."

He looked so damned familiar, sitting there with his eyes alight with laughter as he teased her. Her old Max, the friend she'd instinctively turned to in her most desperate hour. Which only made it even more confusing that five minutes ago she'd been ready to jump his bones.

"Tell you what. Why don't I take care of dinner? In the interests of it being edible," he said.

She stared at him, utterly bewildered. Why was she suddenly having these feelings for him, after all these years?

"Fine. I'll buy some wine," she said.

She grabbed her purse and headed for the door. Out in the street, she blinked and wrapped her arms around her body.

She had to get a grip. Stop thinking about Max in any terms other than as a friend, and start thinking like a normal person.

A normal, really, really cold person. She shivered and hugged herself tighter. It was damned frigid, and she was too used to the blue skies and searing heat of home.

A normal person would go buy herself a coat rather than stand freezing in the street. A coat, some shoes and maybe some jeans. And, while she was at it, some underwear and toiletries.

She kept herself occupied with a mental shopping list as she walked along the cobblestone street and out into the main thoroughfare. Traffic whizzed past as she looked left, then right. She shrugged. It didn't matter where she went. She was just getting away from Max. She knew Paris well enough to know that she would find good shopping no matter which direction she headed.

Within an hour she was bundled in a full-length black wool coat, a long, brightly striped scarf and a stylish scarlet wool cap that covered her ears and reflected some color onto her pale face. She found jeans, a pair of low-heeled black ankle boots she could wear with pants or a skirt, underwear and various other essentials at the huge BHV department store on Rue de Rivoli. Twice she forced herself to put down small items that caught her eye for Max. A scarf the exact color of his eyes. A pair of gloves made from the softest calfskin. Today was not a day to buy gifts for Max.

After she was satisfied that she had enough to survive a week or two, she rode the escalators to the top floor and sat in a corner of the vast cafeteria nursing a cup of watery, burned-tasting coffee.

She didn't want to go home yet. She stared out over Paris,

her mind zigzagging between worrying over her inappropriate attraction to Max and speculating about her appointment with Dr. Rambeau. He had to give her hope. He had to have a magic rabbit to pull out of his hat. If he didn't... She couldn't let herself go there.

She left the department store and struck out aimlessly into the winding streets of the third arrondissement. Her shopping bags banged her calves as she meandered blindly past colorful window displays.

She was about to seek refuge from the cold in a bistro when the passionate, hip-swinging beat of Latin music met her ears. She followed the music down a busy side street and beneath an archway into a cobbled courtyard. A tall, whitewashed building surrounded her on three sides, the ground floor of which was open to the world thanks to large floor-to-ceiling windows. She stared into a wooden-floored dance studio, filled with brightly clad women in various interpretations of Spanish flamenco costumes. Frills and lace and full skirts, petticoats, fishnet stockings—one woman even had a mantilla in her hair. A teacher stood in front of them, demonstrating a move.

Maddy watched with a smile as they all began to dance, feet stomping, fingers clicking and curling and gesticulating, skirts swirling as they spun. They weren't all good. Some were very bad, in fact. But that was beside the point. They felt the music. They were having fun.

She'd always loved Latin. When she'd first started out as a professional dancer, she and her friends would seek out the small Latin-American nightclubs in Sydney's inner city and spend the night dancing for fun instead of perfection and achievement. Max used to come with them, she remembered. She'd loved matching her moves to his to the demanding beat of a rumba or samba. She couldn't remember the last time she'd danced for fun, until she was sweaty and laughing and exhausted. Too long. Even before her injury her life had become so defined by her career and her position within the company that her world had shrunk to rehearsal, performance and more rehearsal.

A particularly bitter gust of wind reminded her that it was too cold to be standing around. She returned to the street, but the rhythm of the music stayed with her. For some reason, she felt calmer, more settled. Ready to go face Max and put the craziness of the past few days behind her.

If she hadn't heard the music and seen the dancers, she probably would have walked right past the dress. She wasn't shopping for frivolities, after all. The vibrant red of roses on a black silk background caught her eye first, then the style of the dress, with its tiny spaghetti straps and buttoned bodice. It had an old-fashioned full skirt, and she could imagine spinning in it, the fabric floating around her. Even though she had nowhere to wear it, she added it to her purchases. It would be a souvenir of her time in Paris.

She stopped at a wine shop then ducked into the *fromagerie* to buy some of the thick, oozing Camembert she knew Max adored.

She was feeling considerably lighter of heart by the time she turned her key in the front door. Time away from Max had given her the perspective she needed. This morning's confusion had assumed its rightful place as a momentary aberration. She was under stress. She'd had an unexpected, explicit glimpse into another side of Max's life yesterday. Combined, the two things had made her silly for a few hours. Nothing more.

He was lounging full-length along the couch reading the newspaper when she entered.

"You're back. I was starting to think I'd have to send out a Saint Bernard."

"I bought some things," she said, holding her bags high to illustrate her point.

"Ah. Silly me. I thought five hours was far too long for any one person to spend looking at shoes."

"Hey! I only bought one pair. And I found a dance school." She dumped her bags beside the coffee table and sank into the armchair. "In this funny little courtyard. There was a flamenco class on. Remember when we used to go to Carmen's and The Latin Bar and dance all night?"

She eased off her shoes and wiggled her toes to relieve the ever-present ache in her feet.

"God, yes. What a pack of show-offs."

It was true. Wherever they went, they'd dominated the dance floor, reveling in their superior skill and flair. She laughed, remembering some of their worst moments.

"We were all so desperate to be onstage. But you're right, in hindsight we must have been pretty obnoxious."

"And the rest."

She reached into her shopping bags and slid the wine and cheese onto the coffee table.

"My contribution, humble as it is," she said.

Max leaned across to inspect the cheese.

"My favorite," he said.

"I know."

He looked surprised, then pleased. She told herself the warm pleasure she felt was just happiness at making him happy. Nothing more.

"I've made us coq au vin for dinner," he said, swinging his legs off the arm of the couch.

"Delicious. I'm starving."

Technically, she needed to be vigilant about what she ate. But it had been cold out, and it wasn't as though she was going to pig out on the cheese alongside Max.

He served the chicken with fresh green beans and baby carrots. She had two glasses of wine and was feeling mellow and sated by the time he pushed back his chair from the table and started to collect the plates.

It's going to be all right, she realized with relief. *This morning is history. We've moved on already.*

The invisible tension that had been banding her chest eased.

"I'll do that," she said, standing and tugging the plates from his hands. "The chef should never have to clean up."

"We'll do it together," he said. "Then you can help me eat this cheese."

"I don't think so," she said with a laugh. "The pâté yesterday was bad enough. No man will ever be able to lift me again if I keep packing it on."

He gave her a reproving look. "Maddy, there's not a spare ounce on you."

"Says the man who doesn't have to fling me around a stage."

They crossed to the kitchen together and he threw her a tea towel after she'd dumped the plates in the sink.

"I hate drying," he said unapologetically.

"Another thing I remember."

"And you hate to vacuum."

"And clean the bathroom. Don't forget that. But I'm great with laundry."

"Together, we almost make the perfect housemate," he agreed.

"Except for forgetting to take the garbage out," she said.

They both laughed.

"Remember the tantrum Jacob pulled that time when we missed the garbage collection two weeks in a row?" she said. Jacob had been one of several dancers who had lived with them.

"Definitely an eleven on the Richter scale."

"Nothing like a gay man for a really good, wall-shaking, knee-trembling tantrum."

He squirted detergent into the sink and reached for the taps.

"Did I ever tell you about the time he tried to seduce me?"

Maddy gave a shout of surprised laughter. "No way!"

"Way." Water shot out of the faucet with a hiss and spray ricocheted off the plates and up into his face.

"*Merde!*" he said, flicking off the taps and wiping water from his face with his hands. "The water pressure in this place is completely screwed. Half the time it's a trickle, then this happens."

"You see? Drying does have its good points," she said with a grin.

He shot her a wry look, then reached for the hem of his soaked T-shirt. Before she understood what he was doing, he'd whipped it over his head. She watched, mesmerized, as he used the balled-up T-shirt to dry his face and mop up any excess moisture on his broad chest. Then he threw the T-shirt to one side and reached for the taps again.

She could barely do more than blink and breathe as she stared at his chest and shoulders and belly. Dark hair curled across his defined pectoral muscles, narrowing down into a sexy trail as it moved south. His jeans rode low on his hips, revealing the hard planes of his abs and the beginning of the delicious, uniquely male groove where his belly muscles met his thighs.

All her hard-won comfort flew out the window. Her mouth was dry. She wanted to reach out and touch him so badly that her fingers clenched into the tea towel. He was beautiful. Perfect. And so damned sexy she wanted to rub herself against him like a cat in heat.

"It was after that party we had when Georgie went off to America. We were all wasted, since we had a long weekend to recover. Remember?"

He was watching her, waiting for her response. She lifted her eyes to his face but was unable to stop her gaze from dropping once more to his chest. He was so male and hot....

"Um. Yeah. That was the party where Georgie threw up in someone's shoe, right?"

He laughed. She stared, fascinated, as his head tilted back on his neck and his belly muscles flexed.

Oh. Boy.

She was in big trouble. Big, big, big trouble.

"I woke up at about four in the morning and Jacob was standing beside my bed, the corner of the sheet in his hand, about to slide in with me. I asked him what he thought he was doing and he said—and I shit you not—'my mother always told me it never hurts to ask.'"

He laughed again. And again his belly muscles did their compelling flex-and-contract thing. She was officially obsessed. And about to do something really, really stupid. She'd never been good at denying her sexual needs. She'd never had to be. She enjoyed sex, and she'd been lucky enough to live and work in a community where she'd never been judged for her appetites. There had been very few men who she'd desired in her life that she hadn't had. She drew the line only at married men—and Max.

But now... Standing so close to his half-naked body, it was difficult to see him as anything but a sexual prospect.

"I told him that if he got into bed with me, he was going to find out that his mom was wrong. Big-time. Then he actually tried to talk me into it. Like he was a car salesman, and all it would take was a bit of good sales patter to get me to change teams."

He shook his head, grinning at the memory. She took a deep breath, then another. She forced herself to take a step backward.

"Jacob always had a thing for you," she said. She could barely recognize her own voice, it sounded so tight and controlled.

"Yeah, it was called a penis."

He passed her the first clean plate, and she almost dropped it she was trying so hard to avoid making contact with his bare skin. One touch. That was all it would take to slip the leash off her self-control right now. He was way, way too sexy and masculine and desirable.

Somehow, they got through the dishes. If Max noticed that she barely lifted her gaze from the floor and that she kept a good few paces between them at all times, he didn't show it. She sighed with relief when he disappeared upstairs afterward and returned wearing another T-shirt.

But to her dismay, it didn't help any. Not enough, anyway. Now she had two images vying for attention in her subconscious—Max in the shower, horny and hard, and Max's chest and belly, up close and personal. Every time she so much as glanced at him both images danced across her mind. Heat fizzed along her veins. Her skin felt sensitized and she could hear her own heartbeat in her ears.

"There's a Godard movie on tonight," he said as he dropped onto the couch, propping his long legs on the coffee table in front of him and palming the remote control. He patted the couch next to him. "Come on. I'll translate for you and tempt you with cheese."

She stared at the couch. There was no way she could survive a whole evening sitting next to him without climbing aboard and taking him for a ride.

She closed her eyes as she imagined his reaction if she tried to enact any of the fantasies running riot in her mind right now. He'd be stunned. He might even laugh at her. Whatever he did, it would be the end of their friendship as she knew it, the comfort and ease between them a thing of the past.

"Let's go out," she suggested.

He frowned. "Out? It's too cold, Maddy. Below zero, in case you hadn't noticed."

Her glance skittered around the apartment, seeking inspiration, and finally landed on her shopping bags. She remembered the dress she'd bought and the flamenco class that had inspired her purchase.

"Let's go dancing," she said. As soon as she said it, she

knew it was right. Dancing was safe. She could churn up the dance floor, get sweaty and breathless in the safety of numbers.

Max was still frowning.

"There must be someplace nearby. Somewhere with Latin-American music?" she asked. God, she was almost begging. She needed some outlet for all the frustration and confused tension building inside her.

"There's The Gypsy Bar. They have dancing. I've been there a few times with a friend of mine," he said.

"Good. Great. Let's do that."

She grabbed the shopping bag with her new dress in it and retreated to the bathroom. She seemed to be spending a lot of her time doing that lately.

Get a grip, Maddy. Get over this. Don't screw up the one good, enduring relationship in your life.

Excellent advice. She just hoped she had the sense to take it.

THE GYPSY BAR was heaving with people and throbbing with loud music as Max pushed open the front door. Maddy bumped into him as he halted to let a couple of women pass by. He stood to one side to make room for her in the crowded foyer. He watched as she tackled the buttons on her coat, knowing already what was beneath it. He'd stared like a tragic schoolboy when she'd stepped out of the bathroom half an hour ago, her new dress swirling around her legs. Slim straps accentuated the delicate lines of her shoulders, while the tight bodice outlined her breasts. He'd known instantly that she wasn't wearing a bra. Her breasts moved with each step, and the gentle, pouting outline of her nipples was visible against the silk.

She was his own personal siren, sent by some higher power to tempt and taunt him. As if it wasn't tough enough to stare at her naked body half the day, wanting what he could never have. Hell, he could still remember the feel of her when he'd hauled her to him to stop her falling this morning. Soft yet strong, her skin warm and velvety, the curve of her breast just the slide of a hand away.

It was getting harder and harder to deny his body's desires. In that respect, her wish to go dancing tonight was a godsend. He needed to let off some steam, release the tension binding him tight.

On the other hand, there was that dress. And the way her hips were already moving in time with the music. It was highly probable that he'd simply traded one form of torture for another.

"Where's the dancing?" she asked, standing on her tiptoes to shout near his ear. The music was so loud the beat reverberated through his heels.

"Up front," he said.

She nodded and immediately began to push her way through the crowd. He followed more slowly and was just in time to watch as she found the edge of the dance floor, filled with gyrating bodies. She didn't hesitate, she simply slid in amongst them and started to move. She'd piled her hair high on her head, leaving wispy tendrils free to hang around her face and shoulders, and she lifted her hands high and shook her head and shoulders and hips in time with the music.

It didn't take long for a man to home in on her, a tall, dark-skinned guy with an appreciative gleam in his eyes. Max watched as they began to salsa together, their bodies locked in rhythm. The other man was smiling with delight at the way Maddy moved in his arms, limber and light and provocative.

Max turned away. He could watch her and go crazy, or he could find his own release in the steamy darkness of the club. He pushed his way to the bar and ordered a cognac. He downed it in one swallow and slid the glass back onto the bar. Then he turned back to the dance floor and let his eyes find her again.

She was spinning, her skirt a swirl of silk around her legs.

She stopped only when her partner reeled her in, her body slamming into his.

"Max. What are you doing here?" He felt a tug on his arm and turned to find a tall slim blonde standing beside him, a surprised smile on her face.

"Marie-Helene," he said. He leaned close to kiss both her cheeks and she caught his mouth in a third kiss before he could pull away. She tasted of wine, and he realized she was a little drunk.

"You haven't called me for an age," she said, cocking her head assessingly. "Have I done something wrong? Worse, have I been replaced?"

He forced a laugh. "I've been busy." He shrugged. They had no ties between them, after all. With Marie-Helene, it had always been about sex and nothing else.

"So you haven't settled down or anything disgustingly boring like that?" she asked, a suggestive smile curling her mouth.

"No."

"Then come dance with me, Max," she said.

She took his hand and led him onto the floor. Eyes holding his, she slid into his arms, their bodies touching from chest to hip. She began to move, and he quickly found the beat.

She was a good dancer, but nothing compared to Maddy. He pushed the comparison from his mind the moment he registered it. This was about forgetting Maddy, losing himself for a few hours.

His step sure, he spun Marie-Helene. She laughed with delight, quickly closing the distance between them so that their bodies were once more pressed together. Her full breasts flattened against his chest, and she ground her hips against his.

If he wanted to, he could go home with her tonight. The invitation was there in every move she made. He could close his eyes and pound into her and find release in her welcoming body.

She smiled, almost as though she could read his thoughts.

She was a generous lover, uninhibited, sensual. But she wasn't Maddy, and he didn't want her the way he wanted Maddy. He wasn't a saint, but the idea of using Marie-Helene as a human scratching post held little appeal.

He wouldn't be going home with her. More fool him, he suspected.

Marie-Helene leaned close to be heard.

"Stop scowling, Max. You look so serious," she said.

The music changed to a fast-moving rumba. He stepped up the pace, turning with Marie-Helene, his hips leading hers.

She laughed with pleasure and at last he felt the music begin to take over, his body following instinctively. This was what he'd wanted, what he'd needed. No thinking, no second-guessing. Just sweat and movement and mindlessness.

A reprieve only—but he'd take what he could get right now.

MADDY TRIED TO STOP herself from watching Max dance with the blond woman. They'd been together for over an hour. She told herself she didn't care what he did, that it was good that he was with another woman. The best thing, in fact. If he went home with her, he'd be well and truly out of bounds. But she couldn't stop herself from watching them.

The way Max splayed his hands over the other woman's hips. The way the blonde pressed her pelvis and her breasts against him. The way she laughed with him, her eyes flashing an unmistakable intimate invitation. There was something about the way they moved together, a certain sure knowledge in their touch that told her they'd been lovers before, that she'd already lain in Max's arms and felt him inside her.

Jealousy burned in Maddy's belly at the thought. Jealousy and envy. Standing on the edge of the dance floor, Maddy toyed with the straw in her drink and tried to make herself look away.

Sweat cooled on her skin now that she was no longer dancing, but her body still hummed with the exhilaration of losing herself—even for a short while—in movement. She'd lost her first partner when he'd suggested they go somewhere more private to dance, her second partner when he'd slid his hand down to cup her ass and she'd slid it back up onto her hip again.

A few years ago, she might have gone home with one of them after a few hours of foreplay on the dance floor. She might have let the excitement and rhythm of moving with a skilled partner spill over into the bedroom. But one-night stands had lost their appeal some time ago. She'd had a series of regular lovers for a while now—successive men who she'd kept at arm's length for as long as possible, then broken off with when it became clear they wanted more than she was willing or able to give.

Across the room, the blonde slid a hand behind Max's neck. Maddy knew what was coming, knew that she should look away, but she couldn't. She watched, her hands clutching around her glass, as the other woman pressed her lips against his. Maddy held her breath as she waited for Max to take up the invitation. After a few taut seconds, he pulled back. She saw the scowl on the other woman's face.

He isn't interested.

Maddy experienced a surge of bone-deep satisfaction. Which was so stupid, she didn't even have the words. But there it was.

She wanted Max for herself.

They were talking now, the woman gesturing toward the bar, signaling she wanted a drink. He nodded and followed her as she fought her way off the dance floor.

The music slid from one song to the next, this one a throbbing, driving salsa. She didn't stop to think. She pushed her way forward and intercepted Max before he disappeared into the crowd near the bar.

She met his eyes, smiled and hooked her finger through one of his. *Just one dance,* she promised herself as she led him back into the thick of things.

He pulled her into his arms the moment they found a spare inch of space. His hips started to move, and she matched his rhythm instantly, easily. One of his hands rested on her hip, the other held her hand, pulling her close. He moved effortlessly, confidently. A sharp, fierce joy hit her. She'd forgotten how good it felt to dance with him.

They danced a salsa, then segued into a rumba. The club was a whirl of lights as Max spun her in his arms. Then the music changed again, switching to a sultry, sexy tango. He pulled her closer again, his hips finding hers, his hand occupying the small of her back.

Locked hip to hip, they strutted across the dance floor. His shirt was damp beneath her hands, clinging to his back. Sweat dripped between her breasts and ran down the column of her spine. Once, twice, three times his thigh inserted itself between hers. Her hand slid from his shoulder to trace his back, then the taut muscles of his arm. His skimmed the top of her backside, his long fingers burning her through her dress. Her breasts tightened, the damp silk of her bodice rasping against her sensually as their bodies moved in unison.

She eyed the column of his throat, watching the pulse that throbbed there. She wanted to press her mouth to his skin. She wanted to taste the salt on his skin and feel the throb of his blood racing through his veins. She wanted to rub herself against him, measure him with her hands and discover if he really was as big and hot and hard as she imagined he would be.

Slowly she lifted her face to his. They locked eyes. Their steps slowed. She didn't stop to wonder if what she was about to do was smart or wise. And she certainly didn't think about tomorrow. She stood on her tiptoes, palmed the back of his neck. Then she kissed him, her tongue tracing the fullness of his bottom lip before sliding into his mouth.

He tasted of brandy and coffee and heat. His tongue met hers, danced with it, stroked it. He pulled her closer. She felt the unmistakable ridge of his erection pressing against her belly. A shiver of need raced through her as she rubbed herself against him.

Max said something in French and his hand swept from her shoulder down to her breast. She arched herself into his palm, her hands gliding over his back to find his butt.

The sudden jostle of another couple backing into them broke their kiss. For a long moment they stared at each other, breathless with need.

Maddy glanced over her shoulder, saw an exit sign. She stepped away from him, linking her fingers with his.

"Come with me," she said.

And she led him outside.

5

THEY EXITED into a small, cobblestone courtyard. A single light illuminated the far corner. She tugged Max into the shadows and pressed herself against him, desperate to finish what they'd started.

He didn't need to be asked twice. His hands cradled her head, his fingers delving into her hair. She heard the faint clatter of hairpins falling to the ground as he kissed her, his tongue sweeping into her mouth. Her hair fell over her shoulders, and he grabbed two fistfuls of it and used it to haul her head back and deepen their kiss.

He pressed closer and she could feel his hard-on throbbing against her stomach. Her whole body was shaking with need. She clutched at his shoulders, digging her fingers into the muscles of his back.

He released her head, one hand shifting to cover her breast, the other to cup her backside. She forgot to breathe as his thumb brushed over her nipple through her dress. She moaned, and he used his grip on her butt to hold her as he ground himself against her. Wet heat throbbed between her thighs, beating out a demanding tattoo.

"Maddy," he whispered, his French accent very pronounced.

He nudged one strap then the other off her shoulders. She felt the coolness of the night air on her bare breasts as he pushed her bodice down. And then he was touching her, cupping her, shaping her, his thumb brushing over and over first one nipple then the other.

She gasped, so turned on she could barely stand. She pulled Max's shirt from his jeans and fumbled for his belt. His hand swept under her skirt. She sucked hard on his bottom lip and slid his zipper down.

Her hand found the hot, hardened length of him just as his closed over the fullness of her butt cheek. He squeezed her once, then slid his hand lower, fingers delving between her legs. Her hand closed convulsively around his thick shaft as his fingers brushed the damp satin of her panties.

"So wet," he whispered roughly.

Then suddenly she was against the wall. Her heart leaped with excitement as Max fisted his hand in the elastic of her panties and pulled. They gave easily and he hitched one of her knees over his hip before both hands found her bare backside. He lifted her and she guided his hardness to her entrance with a shaking, desperate hand even as she locked her ankles together around his waist.

She gasped as he plunged inside her to the hilt. It was almost painful he was so big, but as soon as he began to move, pleasure vibrated through her body in overwhelming waves.

"So good," she murmured, throwing her head back. "So good."

He tightened his grip and began to pump into her in earnest. The slick length of him sliding in and out of her, the granite hardness of his body straining toward hers, the demanding passion of his kisses—she couldn't get enough of him. Then he lowered his head and sucked a nipple into his mouth. His tongue teased, taunted. She dug her fingers into his shoulders and offered him everything she had.

Tension spiraled tight inside her. Sensation rippled through her body. It was all so good. Any second now she would find what her body was chasing. Closing her eyes, she gave herself over to the madness.

She was incredible. So tight and hot and wet. Each thrust into her body, each taste of her sweet nipples, each moan that eased from her throat pushed him nearer to the edge. She was everything he'd ever imagined and more. So soft, her skin so silken, the muscles beneath so sleek and strong.

He couldn't get enough. She felt so good, so right. He wanted to stay inside her forever, but he also wanted to lose himself, to make her lose herself.

He switched his attention from her left breast to her right. Her nipple was already sitting up, begging for his attention. She was the sexiest woman in the world.

He pulled her nipple into his mouth, sucked on it hard. She started to pant. He soothed his tongue over her, then bit her gently. She gasped and writhed. She was close. He could feel her tightening around him. He stepped up the pace, plunging in and out of her, holding on, holding on, no matter how tight and wet she felt, no matter how badly he wanted to find his own climax.

She started to shudder. Her head fell back on her neck. He switched focus to her other breast, sucked hard on her nipple, laving it all the while with his tongue. Her whole body tensed, her spine arching, her hips pushing toward him. Then she was pulsating around him, her inner muscles throbbing.

He gave up the fight to hang on. She was too much. Too hot, too slick and needy and tight. He groaned as his climax roared through him. He nestled his face into her neck, inhaling the scent of her as pleasure washed through his body.

Maddy. So beautiful. So sexy. His at last.

He wanted it to last forever, but his thighs and arms were burning with the effort of supporting both their weights. He withdrew from her reluctantly. She unlocked her ankles and he lowered her to the ground. The moment he stepped away from her, the coldness hit him.

He couldn't see her face clearly in the darkness. She pulled up the bodice of her dress. Then she ducked down and he realized she was collecting her underwear.

Right.

The sweat from the dance floor and their frantic coupling was turning to ice on his back and chest.

"It's cold," he said.

"Yes." She wrapped her arms around her torso. He still couldn't see her face.

"Better get inside."

They turned toward the door. She led the way, dragging the heavy fire door open. The heat and noise of the nightclub hit them like a wall as they stepped inside. Maddy stopped in her tracks, looking lost and overwhelmed.

"Come on," he said, taking her hand.

He pushed through the crowd, towing her behind him. It wasn't until he was holding her coat for her in the cloakroom that he saw the marks on her back.

Red welts, abrasions from where he'd pushed her against the wall.

He swore under his breath as Maddy buttoned her coat to the collar and began to wind her new scarf around her neck.

He'd hurt her. He'd been so wild to get inside her, he hadn't thought of anything else.

They were silent as they stepped into the street. He watched his breath mist in the cool night air. He didn't know where to start.

"Are you okay?" he asked.

She hunched into her coat.

"Can we do this at home? Please?"

He eyed her for a beat. She turned away and started walking. He caught up with her in two strides. The streets were empty and silent as they made their way through the maze of Le Marais to his loft.

Their footsteps sounded loud on the wooden floor as they entered. He stopped in the living area. Maddy hovered nearby, not quite meeting his eye.

"Did I hurt you?" he asked.

"I'm fine."

"At least let me look at your back."

"I told you, I'm fine."

"Then let me see it."

She stared at him, on the verge of protest.

"If I hurt you, I want to know about it," he said roughly.

"You didn't hurt me, Max," she said. But she shrugged out of her coat and offered him her back. "It's nothing, see?"

He stared at the raised, red marks on her pale skin. In good light, he could see they were more irritation than abrasion. He lifted his gaze to the long, slender column of her neck, bowed before him. There were so many things he wanted to say.

"Maddy, what just happened—" He broke off as she pulled away from him.

"I can't do this right now, Max. I'm sorry."

Without looking at him, she strode for the bathroom. He stared at the door as she closed it between them. After a few long seconds, the shower came on.

He closed his eyes.

Great. She was washing him off her skin. Couldn't wait to do so, in fact.

In all the years that he'd fantasized about having sex with Maddy, not once had he imagined what would happen afterward.

Not this, that was for sure.

MADDY SAT on the closed toilet lid, her head in her hands. Steam from the shower filled the room. She'd turned the water on the moment she entered, hoping the sound would convince Max she was taking what had happened between them in her stride.

She'd screwed up. Badly. She'd seen something she'd wanted, and she'd reached out for it like a greedy child. And now she had to face the consequences.

"Idiot, idiot, idiot," she said under her breath.

She'd seen the questions in Max's eyes. He wanted to know why she'd kissed him. Why she'd rubbed herself against him and pushed herself into his hands and led him outside.

He kissed you back. He wasn't exactly resisting.

She groaned, pressing her fingertips against her closed eyelids until she saw stars.

Of course Max had kissed her back. She'd practically ravished him, climbing all over him, grinding herself against him. He would have had to pry her off with a crowbar and a bucket of water she'd been so turned on and desperate for him.

Her stomach was churning. She swallowed, the sound loud in the small space.

She couldn't take back any of it—the kiss, the trip outside to the courtyard, those hot, hard, fast minutes when nothing else had mattered. Worse, even at the height of her regret and shame and remorse, she wasn't sure she would, even if she could. Those few breathless moments with Max would stay with her forever. She'd never been so wild for a man before.

And yet Max was her friend. She loved him with all her heart for his generosity of spirit and his easy sense of humor and his strength and cleverness. She didn't want to mess up what she had with him. She absolutely did not want to hurt him or make him angry or disappoint him. And in her experience, sex came hand in hand with all of the above.

So why had she risked everything by crossing the line with him?

The bathroom was so thick with steam her dress was damp and her hair heavy with moisture. She stood and used her hand to clean condensation from the mirror. The face staring back at her was tight with confusion and guilt.

She pulled off her dress, letting it drop to the floor. She stepped under the shower and thrust her head beneath it, lifting her face into the flow. For long seconds she let the water sluice over her. Then she reached for the soap and began to wash her body. Her breasts tightened as she smoothed the bar of soap across them and she remembered Max's touch on her skin. She washed the sticky warmth of their mutual desire from between her thighs and she remembered his fingers gliding inside her. She bit her lip, torn between desire and regret.

She shut off the water and wrapped herself in her towel.

The apartment was dark and silent when she exited the bathroom. Max had gone to bed.

Her shoulders relaxed a notch. She made her way to her bed and found Max's old T-shirt beneath her pillow. She tugged it on, then crawled beneath the covers and closed her eyes.

Her body was as stiff as a board, and her back had begun to sting.

The scent of Max rose from his T-shirt to envelop her, just as it had last night and the night before. She pressed her face into the pillow. Tomorrow she would buy a pair of pajamas and stop surrounding herself with Max.

God, tomorrow.

She tried to imagine what might happen, what Max might say in the cold light of day, what she could say to make everything right between them, but she knew there was no easy solution.

They'd crossed the line. More correctly, she'd crossed the line and dragged Max with her. And tomorrow, she was going to have to pay the piper.

She thought of all the lovers she'd lost over the years.

I don't want to lose you, too, Max.

But it was possible she already had.

MAX WOKE EARLY. For a second he stared blankly at the wall beside his bed. Then memory returned in a hot, sticky rush.

Maddy against the wall, thrusting her hips toward his. Maddy's breasts pouting in his hands. Maddy whispering her pleasure in his ear.

Then the aftermath: her injured back; the walk home; the way she'd disappeared into the shower.

He had a flash of the stunned, bewildered look she'd had on her face when they stepped back into the nightclub. At least he'd had ten years of knowing he desired her. What had happened last night seemed to have taken Maddy completely off guard.

And yet...

It had happened. She'd wanted him. She'd invited him to dance with her, and she'd teased him with every move she made. Then she'd kissed him. And led him outside.

She'd wanted him. That much was a reality, even if he'd taken over from there, slamming her against the wall and losing it a little as he pounded himself into her.

He ran his hands over and over the short bristle of his hair, staring at the ceiling. Then he rolled out of bed. He descended the stairs quietly, reluctant to wake Maddy before he was ready to face her.

Given what had happened, there was something he needed to take care of this morning. Something he should have done yesterday, perhaps even the day before.

After a quick shower, he dressed and slipped outside to make a few phone calls without disturbing her. He paused near her bed when he reentered the apartment, his cheeks tingling from the cold outside. Her back was to him, her hair tangled on the pillow.

He could still feel the silk of it sliding through his fingers last night.

He forced himself to keep walking. In the kitchen, he quietly prepared breakfast for one.

He was standing at the table reading the newspaper when he heard her stir. He looked over as she sat up, pushing her hair off her face. She looked flushed and soft. Very sexy and kissable. He quickly returned his attention to the newspaper.

He flicked the page over and concentrated on a story about student protests at the Sorbonne and didn't allow himself to look up again until he heard the scuff of her footsteps. She stopped a few feet away and eyed him uncertainly.

Her face was pale, tense. They stared at each other for a long, drawn-out beat. Then Maddy made an inarticulate sound and crossed the distance between them. He froze as her arms slid around him and her body pressed against his. She held him tightly, her cheek resting on his chest. After a fraction of a second's hesitation he returned her embrace.

"I'm so sorry," she said. "I should never have kissed you like that last night."

Her words were muffled, she was holding him so tightly.

"I don't even know why it happened. You mean too much for me to screw up our relationship with sex. We've been friends for so long, and I value you so much. You're one of the few people I can rely on the in the world and I don't want it to change things between us."

He could hear the tears in her voice. Her body was trembling with emotion. He hated seeing her so upset.

"It's okay, Maddy." He lifted a hand to smooth her hair.

She lifted her face to look at him. Her eyes were shiny with unshed tears.

"I don't want to lose you, Max."

"You haven't. It was one night."

"I don't even know why it happened," she said again.

He squeezed the nape of her neck, then eased out of her embrace.

"You're freaking out over your career, under pressure. And

I've got some shit going on, too. We were just letting off steam," he said.

It was the rational, sensible take on what had happened. A version of events that gave them both a get-out-of-jail-free card.

She studied his face, her brow furrowed. Whatever she saw there seemed to reassure her, because her frown slowly faded.

"Thank you," she said. The tears were back then, and she blinked rapidly.

"We were both there, Maddy. Last time I looked, it still took two to do what we did," he said. "Stop blaming yourself."

"When you've ruined as many relationships as I have, it's hard not to. I mean, I'm kind of the common factor."

She offered him a self-aware half smile.

He needed something to do with his hands, something to distract him from how vulnerable and sexy and appealing she looked, standing there wearing his T-shirt, apologizing for having had sex with him last night.

"You want a coffee?"

"No, thanks."

She sat at the table while he remained standing. He poured himself a coffee and added milk. She reached for the sugar bowl and began fiddling with it, twisting it around and around on the table. When she spoke, he saw there was color in her cheeks.

"There's something else I wanted you to know, too," she said in a rush. "I'm on the pill. And I always use condoms, so you don't need to worry about anything. Just in case you were worried, I mean."

He stared at her. Protection had been about the furthest thing from his mind last night. Score another point for Team Stupid.

"Same goes," he said, his voice coming out a little gruff. "I'm always careful."

She nodded, twisting the sugar bowl around a few more

times. "Good. That's that settled. Now we never have to talk about it again." She smiled to show she was joking, then stood. "I'd better get dressed, I guess."

He watched her walk away, noting the straight column of her spine, the elegant arch of her neck, the grace of her movements.

The bathroom door closed between them and he let out the breath he'd been holding. Then he put down his coffee cup, braced his hands on the table in front of him and let his head drop.

He swore under his breath in French and English. For good measure, he threw in a couple of Spanish curses he'd picked up over the years.

He was an idiot, ten times over. All the bullshit he'd fed himself about only being physically attracted to Maddy. All the justifications for his need for her, his desire to protect her and make her happy and ease her pain.

He loved her. Had probably never stopped loving her.

And she only saw him as a friend. Same old, same old.

Shit.

IT'S GOING TO BE ALL RIGHT.

Her eyes felt gritty, and her head ached, but it was going to be all right. Max had let her off the hook. Or maybe he'd let them both off the hook. Whatever. They'd survived the morning after, their friendship intact.

She wasn't stupid—she knew it would be weird between them for a day or two. But they'd get over it. If it killed her, they'd get over it. She'd made a stupid, impulsive, indulgent mistake, and she was determined to put things back the way they should be.

She brushed her hair and dressed in the slim-fit jeans and grass-green turtleneck sweater she'd bought the previous day. She brushed her teeth, took one last look at her pale reflection, then reached for the door.

"Max, you've officially ruined me. I can't stop thinking about bread," she said.

She stopped in her tracks. Max had a visitor. She was tall and slim with wavy shoulder-length auburn hair and very fair skin, and she was standing in the kitchen having coffee with Max. Maddy guessed she was about twenty-two, maybe a little younger. Her gaze dropped to the other woman's feet, noting the distinctive, giveaway turnout of her toes.

A dancer. Maddy's stomach dipped. She could think of only one reason why another dancer would be standing in Max's kitchen.

"Maddy, come and meet Yvette. She's a friend of Gabriella's. She's agreed to model for me," Max said.

For a moment she couldn't breathe. Max had replaced her. And not in the last ten minutes, either—he wouldn't have been able to conjure another dancer out of thin air just like that. While she'd been fretting and agonizing over what last night meant to their friendship, Max had been quietly, coolly working to replace her.

The other woman was wide-eyed as she stared at Maddy.

"Ms. Green, I am very excited to be meeting you. I could not believe it when Max said you were staying with him. I saw you dance in Berlin two years ago. Your Juliet was so wonderful... I'm sorry, I do not have the words," Yvette said in heavily accented English.

"Thank you. That's very kind," Maddy said. She even managed a smile.

"Not kind at all. Simply the truth," Yvette said.

Maddy could feel Max watching her.

"This way you'll have more time to do your strength training and work on your recovery," he said.

Yvette looked concerned, her gaze darting between the two of them.

"You have an injury, Ms. Green? Not a serious one, I am hoping?" she asked.

"Nothing to worry about," Maddy said. She wasn't about to discuss her knee with the other woman. She already felt exposed enough as it was.

"That is a relief. The world of ballet cannot afford to lose you yet," Yvette said earnestly.

Maddy smiled again, even though her face felt tense.

Max turned to Yvette. "The only thing we have left to discuss is your start date," he said.

Maddy crossed to her bed, sitting on the edge to pull on her socks and boots. Her hands were shaking. She took a deep breath to steady herself.

"I am not working, so it is up to you," Yvette said.

"Well, the sooner the better for me."

Maddy grit her teeth. She wanted to pick up her boot and throw it across the room at him.

"I could come tomorrow. Or I have my dance bag in the car right now if you want to start this morning…?" Yvette offered.

"Yeah? That'd be great. Means I won't be off my schedule," Max said.

Maddy allowed herself one glance toward the kitchen. Yvette was leaning against the table, hands braced behind her, long legs stretched out in front of her. Unable to help herself, Maddy eyed the other woman's chest. She was a good cup size larger than Maddy. A lot younger, too. And she had the kind of legs men dreamed of getting tangled in.

Because she was a glutton for punishment, Maddy switched her attention to Max.

He had his hip cocked against the kitchen counter, one hand tucked into the front pocket of his jeans. His jaw was shadowed with stubble and his shoulders looked ridiculously wide in a black fine-knit sweater. There were no prizes for guessing why

Yvette was so keen to be accommodating. Max was sex personified standing there in his bare feet and faded jeans.

"I shall get my things from my car," Yvette said brightly.

She headed for the door. She was very tall, Maddy decided as she watched the other woman walk away. Too tall for classical ballet. Maddy felt a small dart of satisfaction. On one front, at least, she had the other woman beat.

Can you hear yourself? Yvette is not *your competition. She will never be the competition because Max is your friend—and that's all he is.*

Still, jealousy burned in her belly, hot and fierce. *She* was supposed to be the one modeling for Max, not some redheaded goddess. Even though continuing to do so would have been strange and awkward and probably very, very unwise after what had happened last night, Maddy hated the thought that he would now be spending hours staring at Yvette's no doubt nubile body.

She stared blindly at her feet, her whole body knotted with tension.

She was officially nuts. One minute she was almost crying with relief that she and Max had managed to recover from last night's transgression, the next she was seething with resentment over another woman.

"Maddy."

She looked up to find Max standing in front of her, his gray eyes watchful.

"I was going to tell you when you got out of the shower, but Yvette arrived earlier than I expected," he said.

"Sure," she said. She even managed a casual shrug. "I understand."

"I know how important your career is to you. The last thing I want is to hold you back by using up all your spare time," he said.

The clatter of Yvette reentering the apartment claimed his attention.

"You can change in the bathroom. There's a robe you can use, if you'd like," he offered, moving away.

Maddy's hands clenched around the bed frame. Now he was offering Yvette his robe—the same robe Maddy had been wearing only yesterday.

She had a sudden vision of how the next few hours would play out—Max and Yvette locked in intense artistic communion as he sketched her naked body, with Maddy lurking on the fringes of the apartment like a female Quasimodo minus a bell tower.

She shot to her feet.

"I'm going out," she said.

Both Yvette and Max looked a little nonplussed by her sudden announcement.

"I need pajamas," she explained. She started winding her scarf around her neck.

"Okay. Don't forget to take the spare key. I might not be around later," Max said.

She nodded, but he was already turning away to organize his supplies. Probably eager to get to the part where he got to stare at Yvette's naked body for hours on end.

She knew she was being unfair, even irrational, but right at this minute her rational self seemed to have checked out of Hotel Maddy.

She had to get out of here before she did or said something stupid—such as going over and kissing Max right in front of the other woman, so Yvette knew to keep her distance.

Nuts. Absolutely crackers.

She grabbed her coat and purse and strode for the door.

"It was lovely meeting you, Ms. Green. An honor," Yvette called after her.

Maddy glanced over her shoulder. Yvette was holding Max's

robe, the deep red silk flowing from her hands, her beautiful face smiling and hopeful.

"You, too," Maddy said, even though it nearly killed her. After all, it wasn't Yvette's fault she was beautiful and limber and sexy. Well, mostly.

Maddy stood in the street and stuffed her hands deep into her pockets, tucking her chin into the folds of her scarf. She had a powerful urge to kick something. Preferably herself.

What was she doing? Sleeping with Max, getting jealous over other women, obsessing over him. He. Was. Her. Friend. When was her thick subconscious going to get the message?

She started up the street, but she hadn't walked more than ten paces before Max called out her name.

Her stomach did an absurd little flip. She swiveled on her heel, her gaze flying to where he stood on the doorstep, the cordless phone in hand.

"My sister wants to know if we'd like to come to dinner tonight," he said.

Maddy stared at him for a long beat, but he didn't say anything else.

"That would be nice," she said.

"Okay. Have fun." He threw her a casual wave before ducking back into the apartment. Maddy stared at the closed door for a long beat.

What had she expected him to say? *Maddy, I'm sorry. The only reason I replaced you is because I can't bear looking at you and not touching you, especially after last night? You're so sexy, I don't know why I never noticed before, you're driving me crazy.*

She made a disgusted sound at her own idiocy. The last thing she wanted was Max making any such declaration because that would mean he cared for her, that he wanted things from her that she didn't have to give. It would be a disaster in the making, the beginning of the end.

Confused, angry, determined, Maddy walked away.

MAX SHIFTED the wine bottle from one hand to the other and wiped his damp palm on the thigh of his jeans. He'd like to blame his clammy hands on condensation on the bottle, but the truth was he was nervous about the night ahead.

He could hear Maddy climbing the stairs to his sister's apartment behind him, the heels of her boots striking the marble steps sharply.

Despite the fact that he and Maddy had lived together for nearly two years, she'd never met his sister. He'd gone to great pains to ensure that was the case—Charlotte was nothing if not perceptive. The last thing he'd wanted or needed was her guessing how he felt about his housemate.

Some things never changed, it seemed.

"I forgot to ask, how did things go with Yvette today?" Maddy asked as she drew alongside him on the landing.

He knocked on his sister's door.

"It was good. Fine. She was a little nervous, but we'll get there."

She wasn't Maddy. She didn't have Maddy's grace or style. But he also didn't feel the stir of arousal every time he looked at her. Yvette was an attractive woman—but she was not the woman he wanted. Consequently, the morning had gone blessedly smoothly. And there had definitely been no need for cold showers afterward.

"Good. I'm glad it worked out."

Maddy smoothed her scarf and tucked a strand of hair behind her ear. She looked nervous, he realized.

"You know, I've always wanted to meet your sister," she said. "Does she look much like you?"

"She has dark hair. But she's a lot prettier."

"I doubt that," she said. Then she bit her lip and looked away.

The door swung open and warm air rich with savory cooking smells swept out to greet them.

"Sorry. I was just taking the soufflés out of the oven. Come in," Charlotte said.

They followed her inside and Charlotte gave Maddy a brief but thorough head to toe as they shrugged out of their coats.

"Charlotte," she said, thrusting out a hand. "Max says you're a dancer, Maddy. From Australia."

"That's right," Maddy said, shaking hands. "Max and I used to live with each other back in the day."

His sister's gaze swiveled around to impale him.

"Max didn't mention that," Charlotte said.

Now Maddy was watching him.

"Didn't you say you just took the soufflés out of the oven?" he asked.

"Merde!" Charlotte said. She took off down the hallway, her high heels skidding on the floorboards.

Max gestured for Maddy to follow his sister into the kitchen.

Half-chopped vegetables were lined up on the kitchen table on a large cutting board, while pots steamed away on the stovetop. Charlotte stood at the counter, frowning at a tray holding three ceramic ramekins.

"The soufflés sank a little," she said critically. "I'm really not happy with this new oven."

He inspected the ramekins. "I'm sure they'll taste exactly the same," he said. His sister prided herself on her cooking and he knew she would give herself a hard time for any small failure.

Charlotte rolled her eyes.

"No, they won't. Being light and fluffy is the whole point of a soufflé. Don't you think, Maddy?"

Charlotte turned to her guest, her interested gaze once again scanning Maddy from head to toe. The first opportunity he got, he was going to tell his sister to cut it out. Maddy was not his girlfriend, and she wasn't there to be cross-examined by his nearest and dearest. Far from it.

"I suppose. Although, to be honest, I'm the last person you should ask about food. As Max will tell you, I can't cook worth a damn," Maddy said.

"Really? Max isn't exactly great, either. Someone will have to learn to cook," Charlotte said meaningfully.

Maddy looked confused for a beat, then her gaze darted to him questioningly.

"Maddy is only staying with me for a week or two," he said.

"Uh-huh." Charlotte looked as though she didn't believe him.

"She has her career to get back to as prima ballerina with the Sydney Dance Company," he clarified.

"Oh." This time Charlotte looked convinced, if disappointed. He could almost see her thoughts and suppositions realigning themselves. God knew what she was going to ask next. He shot Maddy an apologetic look and she smiled faintly.

"So, how are you finding Max's new apartment, Maddy?"

"Um, good. I mean, I didn't see his old one, so I can't compare, obviously. But it's very nice. Lots of space," Maddy said.

"I wouldn't know," Charlotte said, nudging Max in the ribs with her elbow. "My brother hasn't invited me yet. How long has it been now, Max?"

"A few weeks," he said repressively.

Charlotte raised an eyebrow and moved to the cutting board.

"Hmmm. Did you look at those course brochures I gave you the other night?" she asked as she started slicing an onion.

Max frowned for a moment, trying to work out what she was referring to. Then he remembered her thrusting them into his hands as he was on his way out the door with the camp bed.

Brochures for degrees in psychology, teaching and occupational therapy, if he remembered correctly. He'd left them all behind in the taxi.

"Haven't had a chance," he said.

Charlotte had been trying to push him into a new career for a while now. He would have to tell her about his artistic ambitions soon, even if only to get her off his back.

"Maybe you can convince him to start thinking about the future, Maddy. I know he deserves a break after all those years of caring for *Père*, but he can't float around forever, wasting his life."

He felt Maddy bristle beside him and had a sudden premonition that things were about to go horribly wrong.

"I'd hardly call Max's art floating around or wasting his life," Maddy said stiffly. "He's incredibly talented and the art world is going to fall on its ass in surprise when he has his first show."

Charlotte's knife froze above an onion.

"Max's art? Sorry?"

Charlotte's gaze shifted between him and Maddy then back again.

Damn. He should have seen this coming the moment his sister issued her invitation. Maddy had been modeling for him, after all. It was only natural that she'd mention it.

"I'm working on some pieces. Sculpture," he explained. "Larger scale, like that figure I did last year."

"And you're going to have a show?" Charlotte asked. The knife still hovered, the point wavering a little in her hand.

"Yes. Hopefully. If I can get some interest," he said.

"I see." Charlotte sent the knife down into the onion with a thunk.

She was hurt. She had every right to be. They were close, she shared all aspects of her life with him. And he'd deliberately shut her out of his because he'd been cautious about openly acknowledging his ambitions.

"I was going to tell you. I just wanted to have more to show you before I did," he said.

Maddy was looking distinctly uncomfortable. "I'm really sorry," she said. "I didn't realize…"

"It's not your fault," Charlotte said, her voice brittle.

"I'm sorry," he said. "I just… I guess I wasn't sure if I could pull it off."

It was the truth, but he could see honesty wasn't going to get him anywhere with Charlotte tonight.

She crossed to the stove and began shoveling chopped vegetables into a pot.

"I understand," she said coolly.

But she didn't, and he knew he had some heavy spadework ahead to soothe her ruffled feathers.

Dinner was tense. Charlotte apologized too many times for the soufflés, then made stiff, overly polite conversation with Maddy throughout the main course.

She resented Maddy for knowing more about his life than she did, he guessed. The age-old instinct to shoot the messenger. He was doing his best to ease the tension when a high-pitched scream echoed through the apartment.

"Eloise," Charlotte said, standing abruptly. "She's been having nightmares lately."

She'd barely taken two steps before Eloise hurtled into the room, her mouth open in another earsplitting scream. Her dark hair, cut in a shorter version of Charlotte's bob, was tangled and matted around her sweaty, tear-streaked face. Her nightgown was damp around her middle, clinging to her small frame. He guessed she'd wet the bed.

"It's okay, sweetie. Mama is here," Charlotte soothed in French, getting down on her knees to scoop Eloise into her arms.

Eloise was so distressed she fought against her mother's embrace, her body bowing backward, her arms and legs thrashing around.

His three-year-old niece had been diagnosed with autism eighteen months ago, and Charlotte fought a constant battle to connect with her youngest child. Early intervention, expensive private therapies and the best nutrition money could buy were all strategies she and Richard were employing in an attempt to improve Eloise's condition, but they could only achieve so much.

"Let her go, Charlotte," he urged his sister quietly. It was clear Eloise could not accept comfort right now, and she would only hurt herself and Charlotte in her distress.

Charlotte reluctantly released her grip and Eloise pushed herself away so violently she staggered. Off balance, she fell onto her back and began to pound the carpet with her heels and fists, screaming all the while at a heartbreaking, stomach-clenching pitch.

He'd seen Eloise like this before, a victim to the overwhelming fear and anxiety that dogged her world, but it never failed to make him feel powerless and pointless.

"Do you have anything you can give her? Something to help calm her down?" he asked.

"She won't keep it down in this condition," Charlotte said wearily.

He put his hand on her shoulder. Watching a loved one in pain was tough enough, but knowing you couldn't even convey your sympathy, love and comfort to them made the burden doubly heavy.

He caught sight of movement out of the corners of his eyes and turned to see that Maddy was quietly clearing the table.

He hadn't told her about Eloise. He'd known the children would be in bed by the time they arrived for dinner, and his sister could be intensely private and prickly about discussing her daughter's condition. More than anything, she hated for Eloise to be an object of pity.

"Don't bother with that," Charlotte said.

Maddy hesitated, then put the plates down.

"Eloise is autistic," he explained quietly.

Maddy nodded. "Is she... Is there anything I can do?" she asked.

"No. She'll have to wear herself out. Fortunately, her body can't sustain such a high level of anxiety for long," he said.

As he spoke, Eloise's screaming dropped in pitch and became a low, despairing moan. She started to rock from side to side, her arms wrapped around her torso.

Charlotte pressed a hand to her mouth and blinked furiously.

"I hate it when she's like this. Out of everything it's the thing I hate the most," she said, her voice low and vehement.

Max pulled his house keys from his pocket and handed them to Maddy.

"Why don't you go on home?" he suggested. "I'll call you a taxi."

"No! There must be something I can do to help," she said.

"If there was, I would be doing it," Charlotte snapped.

Max made eye contact with Maddy. She nodded her understanding of his silent message.

"Okay. I'll go, if that's what you think is best," she said quietly. She took the keys from him, but hesitated, clearly uncertain about whether she should thank her hostess before leaving.

Charlotte didn't lift her gaze from Eloise's rocking form and Maddy turned away. He followed her to the door and helped her on with her coat.

"I'm sorry," he said when she faced him. "Charlotte's under a lot of pressure."

Maddy held up a hand. "Don't. I'm fine. I completely understand."

In the other room, Eloise started screaming again.

"Go," she said, urging him back. "I'll see you at the apartment."

She squeezed his arm, then she was heading down the stairs, her footsteps echoing hollowly in the stairwell.

Charlotte was holding Eloise in her lap when he returned to the living room.

"I suppose we shocked Little Miss Prima Donna. Not quite what she's used to."

"Charlotte."

"Don't think I don't know what she was thinking. That I'm a terrible mother or I can't cope or—" Charlotte's voice broke and she tightened her grip on her daughter.

"Will she take some hot milk now?" he asked.

He wasn't about to defend Maddy to his sister. They both knew that Charlotte wasn't angry with Maddy. It was simply much harder to rail at life in quite the same way.

"Maybe. We can try."

By the time he'd returned with warm milk, Eloise had quietened. Half an hour later, Charlotte carried her to her room to tuck her into bed. Eloise was limp with exhaustion by then, her eyes puffy from crying.

Max cleaned up the kitchen while Charlotte sat by Eloise's bedside, waiting for her to fall asleep. He was wiping down the counters when Charlotte spoke from the doorway.

"Do you still love her?"

He stilled.

"You think I didn't notice, all those years ago? The way you talked about her, then carefully tried to make it sound as though you weren't, in case I noticed? You think I didn't understand that you were trying to stop me from meeting her?" Charlotte said.

"Stop it, Charlotte. Maddy is not the one you're mad at, and you know it," he said.

His words came out more firmly than he'd intended and Charlotte shut her jaw with a click and stared at him as though he'd slapped her. He crossed the room to draw her into his arms. Even though she remained stiff and angry, he kissed her forehead.

"I'm sorry for not telling you about my plans," he said quietly, trying to find the right words. "It wasn't because I don't care about what you think. I guess I just wasn't sure if I was doing the right thing."

Some of the fight went out of her.

"You know I love your bronzes. How could you think I would be anything but supportive?"

He shrugged. "It's not exactly a reliable career choice."

"So? I want you to be happy. That's all I've ever wanted for you."

He kissed her forehead again.

"Can I come around to your apartment now that the big secret is out?"

"Of course. I wasn't deliberately keeping you away, Charlotte," he said.

She pulled away from his embrace and gave him a knowing, sisterly look.

He shrugged. "Okay, maybe I was, a little."

"You didn't have any trouble telling Maddy, showing Maddy."

"She turned up on my doorstep. It was kind of hard to avoid it."

"That's not why you told her. You love her."

This time he didn't bother to deny it.

"She's very beautiful," Charlotte said.

He just raised an eyebrow. "We're friends. Nothing more."

"Prove it to me. Go out with one my friends. Luisa has been waiting to meet you for months."

"No." The answer was on his lips before he could even think about it.

There was only one woman he wanted. More fool him.

Charlotte shook her head. "I hope you know what you're doing, Max."

He already knew that he didn't. He'd let Maddy back into his life in every conceivable way—into his home, his art, his bed, his heart. And, as always, she had no idea how profound an impact she'd had on him.

For a brief moment he regretted finding her on his doorstep four nights ago. Then he remembered the sweet, searing heat of being inside her. The soft, needy sounds of her desire. The silk of her hair in his hands.

It made him ten different kinds of idiot, but he wouldn't trade that experience for anything in the world.

Which only proved he really was a glutton for punishment.

6

Maddy pulled on her new pajamas when she got home and curled up on the couch to wait for Max. She'd hated leaving before him, but it had quickly become clear that it would be easier for both Charlotte and Max if she were gone.

Max's sister didn't like her.

Maddy had had people not like her before—temperamental choreographers, ambitious dancers keen to usurp her position, angry ex-lovers—so it wasn't as though being the object of someone's enmity was new to her. She was surprised by how much Charlotte's reaction hurt.

She'd wanted so much for Max's family to like her. Over the years, she'd often heard him talk about Charlotte. For some reason, they had never run into each other until now. Still, Maddy had always imagined that if ever they did meet, the connection between them would be as effortless and instant as it had been with Max.

Nice idea, shame about the reality check.

Charlotte had started assessing Maddy the moment she stepped over the threshold, and things had gone downhill rapidly when she stepped in to defend Max's fledgling art career. Maddy winced as she recalled the utter surprise and hurt on Charlotte's face when she'd understood her brother had been holding out on her.

Her thoughts shifted to Eloise, Max's niece. Maddy was the first to admit she had next to no experience where children were concerned. But she knew enough to recognize that she had not witnessed a normal, everyday kind of tantrum and that Eloise had special needs. Maddy wondered why Max hadn't mentioned earlier that his niece was autistic. Did he not trust her with the information?

Maddy's stomach tightened as she recalled the high, distressed pitch of the little girl's cries. That Charlotte had been unable to connect with her or comfort her… Maddy could only imagine how the other woman must have felt. How powerless and angry and sad.

A knock at the door pulled her out of her thoughts. She crossed to let Max in.

"Thanks," he said as he stepped across the threshold.

She wrapped her arms around herself and followed him as he moved into the living area. "Did Eloise settle down okay?" she asked.

"Yeah. She's back in bed, dead to the world. Absolutely exhausted."

He peeled off his coat and rolled his shoulders. He looked tired.

"Can I get you a drink? Some cognac? Hot chocolate?" she asked.

He shook his head. "Look, I wanted to explain about Charlotte."

"Max, you don't need to. As I said back at the apartment, I totally understand."

"She's not normally like that. Her husband, Richard, has to travel a lot with his work, so she's alone with the kids most of the time. Lately, it seems to have really been getting her down, but I'm not sure—" He broke off and smiled ruefully. "Sorry. This is probably the last thing you want to talk about after the night you've had."

"Of course I want to talk about it. You're worried about her, aren't you?"

"She's got a lot on her plate. And she never asks for help until she's pushed to the limit."

Maddy sat on the couch, drew her knees up to her chest and rested her chin on them.

"Tell me about Eloise," she asked quietly.

She wanted to know about Max's world, about the people he cared about. More importantly, she wanted to ease the worried crease that had formed above his eyebrows. She wanted him to feel he could share his burdens with her, the way she'd shared hers with him.

He sat opposite her.

"What do you want to know?"

"How old is she? How long have you known she's autistic?"

"She's three. She had the first tests about eighteen months ago, but Charlotte already suspected something was wrong. Eloise was speech delayed, and she hardly ever made eye contact."

"I don't know much about autism," Maddy admitted.

Max explained that there was still a lot of debate about what caused autism, and that patients were diagnosed on a spectrum. Some children grew up to have close to normal lives, while others remained profoundly isolated.

"Where does Eloise fit in?"

"It's too early to judge. She's responding well to early intervention, but there are no guarantees."

"She was so upset," she said.

"Current theory is that most autistic children are profoundly anxious a lot of the time. That's why they respond well to routine—and badly to any break in it."

"Right. That makes sense, I guess."

Max yawned and stretched.

"I'm keeping you up," she said guiltily.

"I probably should turn in," he said, standing. "Yvette's coming around early tomorrow."

Right. Yvette.

"Good night," she said.

He smiled faintly and headed for the bathroom. She watched him walk away.

She fought a sudden urge to race after him and put her arms around him. It seemed wrong that they would be sleeping in separate beds tonight when he was clearly troubled and in need of support. In the old days, if she'd thought he was upset or worried about something, she'd have come up with an excuse to crawl into bed with him.

Things had been a lot less complicated back then.

That's because we hadn't had sex.

It was true, but it was also less than the truth because what was going on between her and Max was about a lot more than just sex.

It was a scary thought, and not one she cared to examine too closely.

Stomach tied in knots, feeling inexplicably lonely, she went to bed.

MAX WOKE TO THE SOUND of humming filtering up from the kitchen below. He rolled out of bed and pulled on a pair of workout pants then headed downstairs. He was shrugging into a T-shirt when he found Maddy slicing a baguette at the kitchen sink. She was showered and dressed and her eyes glowed with suppressed excitement when she greeted him.

"Guess what? Nadine called—finally—and she's recovering from surgery herself."

"That's too bad. Is she all right?"

"A bunion, nothing major," Maddy said. "Guess who her doctor is?"

"Let me see… Someone good? Who she can get you an appointment with?"

She threw the dish towel at him.

"Not just *someone*. Dr. Kooperman. The best of the best." Maddy pressed her hands together. "I mean, Dr. Rambeau was great, but Dr. Kooperman! I'm pinching myself. Nadine has a follow-up appointment with him today, but she's going to ask him if he will see me instead. Isn't that amazingly generous of her?"

He'd heard of Kooperman. Most dancers had. He was long established, an early pioneer in dance medicine.

"Fantastic. Great news," he said.

Even though it meant Maddy was one step closer to leaving.

"I know. I can't believe it. Nadine called about an hour ago, and I've been jumping out of my skin ever since, dying to tell you. If I had to wait for an appointment the normal way, it would be months and months before he could see me."

She was so energized it made him realize how subdued she'd been ever since she'd arrived. For a moment he was afraid for her. If she didn't get the news she wanted from these specialists...

"I made you breakfast," she said, sliding toasted slices of baguette toward him.

"What time is your appointment?" he asked as he sat.

"I'm not sure. Nadine needs to check that it's okay with the doctor before she hands over her appointment time."

She sat opposite him as he spread jam on his toast. Her right leg jittered up and down nervously, her foot tapping on the floor so fast it was practically vibrating.

"This could be it, Max. He'll probably want to run some tests, but if he gives me good news, I can ring Andrew and force him to reinstate me."

"You won't need to force him, Maddy. You're their star attraction."

She shrugged a shoulder. "There's always someone waiting in the wings. You know that. But they'll have to honor my contract if I get the all clear."

She'd practically packed her bags and boarded the plane

already. He concentrated on his toast, making sure he spread the jam right to the edges. She'd only been back in his life for a few short days but she'd leave a huge hole when she left.

He gritted his teeth. He'd played the missing Maddy game before. He wasn't looking forward to round two. He had a feeling it was going to be even more brutal the second time around. He'd slept with her, after all. He knew exactly what he was missing.

Aware that Yvette was due to arrive at any moment, he finished eating then crossed to his work area to set up his equipment and turn on the extra heater. Maddy began to clean the kitchen, once again humming beneath her breath.

"I was thinking that maybe I could call Charlotte today to thank her for dinner," she said after a while.

He glanced up from his sketch pad.

"Probably not a great idea," he said.

"Oh."

She straightened the salt and pepper shakers on the table.

"Maybe I could buy Eloise a gift, then?"

"To be honest, I think it's probably best to just let Charlotte find her equilibrium."

"She really doesn't like me, does she?"

He considered lying, but they'd both been there last night.

"She doesn't know you. What happened last night was about me not telling her something she felt she had a right to know and Charlotte being stressed. You happened to be standing nearby when the shit hit the fan."

"Hmmm."

The sound of frantic knocking at the front door had his head snapping around.

"Max!"

It was his sister's voice, strident with emotion, and he reached the door in two strides.

"M-Max!" Charlotte stuttered the moment she saw him, her face crumpling. "Marcel has hurt himself at school. They said he fell down some stairs and hit his head and they rushed him straight to hospital."

She was trembling. Max put an arm around her.

"It's all right. Take a deep breath," he said.

He waited until she'd done so before talking again.

"Which hospital?"

"Hôtel Dieu," she said. "I'm going over now, but I can't take Eloise. She'll get too upset, and I need to be there for Marcel."

"I'll take her," he said instantly, guessing that was what she wanted.

Charlotte's eyes filled with tears.

"Thank you! Oh, thank you. I wish Richard was here. I need him. If something happens to Marcel—"

"Nothing will happen to him. Have you called Richard? Is he coming home?" He knew his brother-in-law was at yet another work conference somewhere in Europe.

"Yes. He was due home tonight anyway, but he's trying to catch an earlier flight."

"Good."

Charlotte was on the verge of tears again. Her car keys were jingling in her hands she was shaking so much.

"After last night... It's too much. I can't keep doing this all on my own," she said in a near whisper.

She sounded exhausted and near the end of her tether. He eyed her with concern, not liking the idea of her driving to the hospital in this condition.

He took her keys and went out to collect Eloise from the car, Charlotte hard on his heels.

"I brought some toys for her, and her favorite DVD," Charlotte explained.

Eloise was playing with a brightly colored prism, oblivious

to the drama around her. Thank heaven for small mercies, he thought as he pulled her into his arms while Charlotte grabbed the bag of toys.

"I don't know how long I'll be. I brought her pajamas, in case I have to stay in the hospital overnight." Charlotte's voice cracked and she started crying in earnest.

Max slid his free arm around her and hustled her back into the apartment.

"I'm going to call you a taxi," he said. "You can't drive like this."

"No! I can't wait for a taxi to come. I have to go now. Marcel needs me," Charlotte said, rising hysteria in her voice.

He hesitated, unsure what to do. He hated the idea of her facing whatever waited at the hospital alone, but someone had to look after Eloise.

"Can I help?"

He swung around to see Maddy standing there, determination writ large on her face. They'd been speaking French, but she clearly understood that something was very wrong.

"I can't be in two places at once," he said, articulating his greatest dilemma.

"No," Maddy said with a frown, and he realized he wasn't making sense.

Quickly he explained the situation to her.

"What if I look after Eloise?" Maddy suggested.

"You've got your doctor's appointment," he reminded her.

Maddy shrugged. "I'll call Nadine. I'm sure Dr. Kooperman can fit me in another time. I want to help, Max."

He looked at Charlotte, saw she was battling to pull herself together, swallowing her tears and straightening her shoulders. She would cope, because she had so many times in the past. But he wanted to be there for her if he could.

"If you don't mind, that would be a help," he told Maddy.

"I'll set you up before we go. Charlotte brought Eloise's favorite DVD. She'll watch it as many times as you play it."

Charlotte blew her nose into a tissue and looked set to wade into the discussion.

"This way I can stay with you," he said, forestalling her.

Charlotte opened her mouth, then closed it again. She nodded.

"That would be nice, I think," she said in a strangled voice.

It took him a couple of minutes to get *Milo and Otis* playing and prop Eloise in front of it.

"If she gets hungry, peanut butter sandwiches are her favorite," he said as he led Charlotte toward the door. "I keep a jar in the kitchen."

Maddy nodded with each instruction. Charlotte dug her heels in on the doorstep and turned to add her own instructions.

"She hates loud music, or any loud noises for that matter. There are spare diapers in the bag. And make sure that you do up all her buttons on her pajamas if we're not home until late. She gets upset if her buttons aren't all done up."

"Okay."

"We'll call from the hospital," Max said as he eased his sister from the house.

Maddy nodded an acknowledgment. She looked small but determined as he shut the door.

He knew exactly how much seeing Dr. Kooperman meant to her, yet she'd given up the opportunity without the bat of an eyelid.

If he hadn't loved her already, that one act of generosity alone would have made him a goner.

If Maddy were his, the life they could build together...

But she wasn't.

Grim, dragging his mind back to Marcel and the task at hand, Max started the car and pulled out into traffic.

As Max and Charlotte disappeared out the door, Maddy turned to study Eloise, bundled on the couch and staring at the television.

Despite what Maddy had said to Max, she was nervous. She knew nothing about children. Nada. Zilch. Zero. As for children with special needs... If something went wrong, she'd be absolutely clueless as to how to respond.

Before her imagination could get carried away drafting potential disasters, she took herself firmly in hand. Eloise was perfectly happy. She was watching her DVD, completely absorbed in the adventures of Milo and Otis. And Max was taking his sister to the hospital, offering Charlotte the support she needed.

Maddy's thoughts shifted to Marcel. He was only six, and he'd fallen down stairs. She felt sick just thinking about it.

One eye on Eloise, she picked up her cell and phoned Nadine. Her friend sounded put out when Maddy told her she wouldn't be able to accept her generous offer of her appointment. Nadine explained that she had already called Dr. Kooperman to ask his permission for the exchange and he had agreed to do so—but not before giving Nadine a hard time. Guilt assailing her from all sides, Maddy outlined the situation as best she could but when she hung up she had the distinct feeling she'd lost her chance at an early appointment with one of France's best dance medicine specialists.

It had been a week since her fateful meeting with Andrew. The longest she'd gone without rehearsing in her life. She felt adrift, totally at sea without the familiar anchors of classes, rehearsals, gym sessions, costume fittings, meetings with choreographers and fellow dancers. She felt like an exile. And she hated it. She wanted her life back.

The familiar panicky dizziness hit her, and she forced herself to take big, deep belly breaths.

Eloise shifted on the couch, pulling at the blanket Max had

wrapped around her. Maddy watched her, taking in her smooth brown hair and intent, serious round face. If Max had children one day, they would look like this, she realized. Dark, with his olive skin.

She shook her head, the moment of panic over. Eloise needed her. Max needed her. And she still had Dr. Rambeau lined up for next week. She would get at least one second opinion, even if it wouldn't carry quite the same ring of authority that Dr. Kooperman's would.

She straightened her shoulders and crossed to the couch to sit beside Eloise. The little girl didn't acknowledge her in any way, not even with the flicker of an eyelid. Maddy sat back to watch the movie.

Milo and Otis were escaping from yet another near-death experience when the doorbell rang half an hour later. It was Yvette. Max had forgotten to call her and cancel their session. Maddy apologized on Max's behalf and arranged for Max to call her to reschedule. To her credit, Yvette was all concern and asked Maddy to pass on her best wishes.

Maddy checked her watch as she crossed back to the couch. Why hadn't Max called? Surely if it was good news, he would have rung by now?

She'd just reset the DVD to play for a second time when her cell phone rang.

"How is Marcel?" she asked.

"He has a bad concussion, and a broken arm. They need to operate to set it, so we're going to be a while," Max said.

"Nothing else?" she asked. She remembered a dancer who had tumbled from the stage a few years ago and fractured his skull. "No pressure or anything from the head injury?"

"They've scanned him, and it all looks normal. He's got one hell of a bruise, though. He was damn lucky."

She sagged with relief. "How is Charlotte?"

"Hanging in there. How are you and Eloise doing?"

"*Milo and Otis* still reign supreme, so I guess we're hanging in there, too."

There was a short pause and she could hear Max take a breath.

"I really appreciate you doing this," he said. "You didn't have to."

"You don't need to thank me, Max," she said. "It was the least I could do."

"But you've lost your chance to see Dr. Kooperman," he said.

"I think your niece and nephew are a little more important than my ability to do a pirouette on stage," she said.

There was a profound silence from Max's end of the line for a few beats.

"Well, both Charlotte and I appreciate it," he said. "We'll have to work out some way to make it up to you."

There was a low, warm note in his voice and her hand tightened around the receiver as a half dozen illicit, wrong, hot ideas for how he could do that flitted across her mind.

"I'd better get back to *Milo and Otis*," she said.

"I'll call later, give you a progress report."

She ended the call and returned to her position on the couch next to Eloise. Once again the little girl didn't acknowledge her presence in any way.

Maddy stared blindly at the television. Her heart was banging against her rib cage as though she'd just danced a solo. Because Max called? Because he'd said nice things to her and made her think about things it was best she never thought about again?

A grinding, clicking noise drew her attention back to the television. The picture was flashing off and on, the image distorted into pixels. She was reaching for the remote control when the machine gave a final mechanical groan and the picture died altogether, the screen cutting to blue.

"Oh, no."

For the first time in two and a half hours, Eloise stirred. She frowned, plucking at her blanket.

"Okay. Okay," Maddy said as she scrambled toward the DVD player.

Maybe the disk had a scratch on it. She pressed the power button on and off a few times, but nothing happened. She could smell a faint burned electrical odor. Not a good sign.

Behind her on the couch, Eloise began to protest. *"Je veux le chat de chat!"*

Maddy's French was rusty, but she got the drift. Eloise wanted her movie back on, pronto.

"I don't think that's going to be possible, *chérie*," she said. "Milo and Otis are having a *petit* sleep."

Eloise was still staring at the television. Her expression darkened ominously. Maddy scooped up the colored prism Eloise had been so fascinated with earlier and handed it to her. Eloise gave it a single disinterested glance before letting it fall to the floor.

"What about lunch? You must be hungry, no?" Maddy tried next. *"Très affamée, oui?"*

She rushed to the kitchen and quickly slapped together a peanut butter sandwich. Eloise became more vocal with every minute, calling out in French for the movie to start again.

"Why don't we eat lunch, first, sweetie?" Maddy suggested, offering Eloise the sandwich cut into quarters.

But Eloise simply wasn't interested. She ignored the plate, pointing at the television. Her voice rising in pitch, she demanded *Milo and Otis*.

Maddy sat back on her heels. She had no idea what to do. Eloise had not made eye contact with her once, and Maddy didn't know if the little girl could understand a word she was saying. Doubtful, given her autism and the fact that Maddy was speaking mostly English with a tiny smattering of French.

Maddy pounced on the bag of supplies Charlotte had brought with her, hauling out pajamas, diapers, some fruit snacks and a well-loved rag doll. She delivered the doll to Eloise with her heart in her mouth, but once again Eloise was not interested.

Just her luck—a kid who knew her own mind.

Eloise's complaints were increasing in volume. Maddy stiffened with alarm as the little girl began to rock. For a split second she considered calling Max, but she didn't want to add more pressure to what was already a stressful situation.

"Okay. It's going to be okay, Eloise," she said soothingly.

She glanced around the apartment, but nothing leaped out at her. In desperation, she did the one thing she was good at—she started to dance.

"Hey, look, *mon petite,* look at this," she said as she did a pirouette, then an arabesque, followed by a deep plié.

She did another pirouette and realized that Eloise had stopped rocking. And for the first time all day, she was focusing on Maddy and following her every move.

A surge of relief washed through Maddy.

"You like this? You like *le ballet?*" She danced a few more steps and noticed that Eloise was moving her arms and legs in abbreviated imitations of what Maddy was doing.

"You want to dance, too?" she guessed.

She danced a few more steps, and again Eloise wriggled in time with her.

"Yes! You do want to dance. What a wonderful idea," Maddy said.

Quickly she located Max's stereo system and shoved the first disk she found into the tray. As Vivaldi's *Four Seasons* poured into the room, she danced toward Eloise and held out her hands.

Her excitement faltered as Eloise simply sat staring at her. Then, slowly, Eloise lifted her hands toward Maddy's and allowed Maddy to pull her to her feet.

Maddy stepped from side to side, encouraging Eloise to copy her. Her tongue wedged between her lips, Eloise rocked back and forth on her chubby baby legs. Once the little girl was moving confidently, Maddy introduced a simple twirl. Eloise's face lit with delight as she whirled in a circle, arms spread wide for balance.

She giggled, her small face flushed with pleasure. Warmth and an odd humbleness filled Maddy as she took in the pure joy on Eloise's face. There was so much honesty there, no pretense or subterfuge or self-consciousness.

"You can feel the music, too, can't you?" she said, even though she knew Eloise could not understand.

Totally immersed in the moment, Maddy began to string a series of simple steps together in her mind. Then, Eloise's hands held fast in her own, Maddy showed her how to dance.

"SHE'LL BE FINE. When I spoke to Maddy they were still watching the DVD," Max said.

Charlotte fretted beside him, hands fiddling with the seat belt as he wove through traffic. Richard had arrived at the hospital half an hour ago. Keen to collect Eloise and take her home, Charlotte had left him to sit with Marcel while Max drove her home. She claimed it was because she knew Eloise hated having her routine interrupted, but Max was aware it had far more to do with Charlotte having taken an irrational dislike to Maddy.

"You know I hate leaving Eloise with strangers," Charlotte said. "It's bad enough when they're trained sitters."

"Maddy's perfectly capable of handling Eloise," he said as they turned into his street.

Charlotte didn't say anything. The moment the car drew to a halt, she was outside and heading for the door to his apartment.

Her expression became grim as she registered the music leaking from his apartment.

"I told her Eloise doesn't like loud noises," she said. "What does she think she's doing?"

Despite his firm belief in Maddy's capabilities, he felt a twinge of concern. He'd seen Eloise howl a dozen times in reaction to anything overly loud.

He opened the door and they both froze on the threshold, surprised into stillness by the sight of Maddy and Eloise dancing together in the center of his work space.

Maddy was leading, her movements simple but graceful, and Eloise was imitating her, pirouetting, leaping, spinning and gliding in a child's interpretation of the choreography. Both were oblivious to their audience, utterly swept up in the moment.

Max's heart squeezed in his chest as he saw how much pleasure Eloise was taking from the experience. Her gray eyes sparkled with delight, and he could hear her laughing above the music.

Charlotte clutched his forearm, her expression torn between shock and amazement. Then Maddy caught sight of them and stopped in her tracks. Her hair had come loose from its topknot and hung in wispy strands around her face and neck. She was flushed, her violet-brown eyes shiny with laughter and fun.

She had never looked more beautiful to him.

"You're back," Maddy said, reaching for the remote control and silencing the music.

Eloise made a noise of protest as she registered that the dancing was over.

"But she hates music," Charlotte said. "I've tried everything. The Wiggles, Disney songs…"

"She loves to dance," Maddy said with a shrug. "She's a natural."

Charlotte shook her head, bemused.

"The DVD player died," Maddy said. "I couldn't find anything else she was interested in, so…we danced."

"You have good instincts. Most autistic children love music and movement. But for some reason Eloise never has," he said.

"Until now," Charlotte said. The look she sent Maddy was searching. "Perhaps she simply didn't have the right teacher."

Maddy shrugged self-deprecatingly. "I didn't do anything special."

Charlotte approached her daughter and knelt so that they were on the same level. Touching Eloise's arm to gain her attention, she held out her arms.

"*Maman* is here," she said with a small smile.

Eloise's mouth quirked to one side in recognition, and she allowed herself to be embraced. Charlotte closed her eyes, savoring the contact.

"How is Marcel?" Maddy asked.

"Out of surgery. Richard is with him. He will have to stay in overnight but with luck he can come home tomorrow," Max explained. "The doctors are very happy with everything, so it seems the worst is over."

"Oh. That's good news," Maddy said with an earnest nod. She tucked a stray strand of hair behind her ear. She looked self-conscious, he realized. Then he understood that she was worried that she'd done the wrong thing with Eloise. Before he could reassure her, Charlotte spoke up.

"I owe you an apology, Maddy," Charlotte said in her forthright way. "I was rude last night. Inexcusably so. I want to thank you from the bottom of my heart for looking after Eloise today, and for making her smile. We don't see enough of that in our house."

She held out her hand for Maddy to shake, and Maddy blinked with obvious surprise before taking it.

"It was my pleasure. We had a lovely time," she said.

"You will have to show me what to do, so Eloise can have a lovely time again," Charlotte said. "And perhaps I could buy you a coffee sometime and we could start again?"

"Of course," Maddy said with a shy smile. "Anytime."

Charlotte looked relieved as she turned to Max. "Thank you for today. I don't know what I would have done without you. I feel like I have been saying that to you a lot lately."

"You know I'm happy to help," he said.

"Still. You have stepped in for us too many times. And I have been pulling my hair out too often. Richard and I will be having some serious talks tonight," Charlotte said solemnly. "Perhaps it is time for him to change jobs."

Max knew that Richard and Charlotte had been walking a fine line the past few years, trying to balance the demands of Richard's high-paying job with the demands of home. They needed the extra income to fund Eloise's early intervention therapies, but Charlotte was clearly reaching the end of her endurance in her role as single parent in all but name.

"Let me know if there is anything else I can do," he said.

His sister flashed him a grateful smile as she began to collect Eloise's things. Maddy extracted the DVD from the broken player and handed it over, then they were out the door, Eloise pressing her face into her mother's neck as Charlotte carried her to the car.

Silence reigned for a long beat after the door closed behind them. Maddy let out a big sigh and flapped the front of her T-shirt.

"Is it hot in here or is it just me?" she asked. "I can't believe Eloise's stamina. She wouldn't let me rest for a second."

He wondered what she would do if he crossed the room and pulled her into his arms and kissed her the way he wanted to right now. She looked so small and strong and sexy standing there. He was fast running out of self-control where she was concerned.

A knock called him back to the front door. It was Charlotte again. She thrust two tickets into his hand.

"Last interruption for the day, I promise. I nearly forgot these. Richard bought them for me for my birthday, but we will not be going to the ballet tonight," she said drily. "You and Maddy go, please. As a thank-you from us both. They will go to waste otherwise."

She flashed Maddy a last smile then was gone again. He studied the tickets. Dress circle, front and center. Good seats.

"What do you think?" he said, glancing at Maddy. "The Garnier Opera Ballet performing *The Nutcracker*?"

"Anna mentioned it when we spoke about Dr. Rambeau," she said. "She's dancing the role of Clara."

He quirked an eyebrow at her, still waiting for an answer to his original question. She nodded.

"Why not?"

"You can glam up. I remember how you like a big event."

"It's been a while since I've been on the other side of the curtain," she admitted.

"I'll take you for dinner afterward," he said impulsively. The idea of wining and dining her held enormous appeal—sitting across a small table from her, sharing good food and fine wine, savoring the flicker of candlelight on her beautiful face. So what if it didn't mean anything and would never lead anywhere? It was a harmless enough self-indulgence, as self-indulgences went.

"You don't have to do that."

"Maybe I want to," he said before he could edit himself.

Awareness crackled between them for a heated moment as they locked eyes. It was the closest he'd ever come to declaring his interest in her. The memory of those few hot moments in the darkness behind The Gypsy Bar hung heavily between them. Maddy broke eye contact, her gaze sliding over his shoulder.

Reality washed over him, cool and undeniable.

You're her friend, remember, idiot? She doesn't want you

looking at her like that or taking her out for intimate dinners or anything remotely romantic.

He shoved his hands into his jeans pockets.

"Maybe we should just have something at home," he said.

"That's probably a good idea."

He bit down on a grim smile. Yeah, he was full of good ideas lately. Just full of them.

MADDY STRAIGHTENED her spine as she climbed the stairs from the Metro station at Place D'Opera in the fourth arrondissement later that evening. Cool night air rushed at her as they stepped from the warmth of underground. She took a moment to absorb their surroundings—the stately buildings, the brightly lit cafés, the art-nouveau streetlights, the well-dressed Parisians rushing past. She swiveled on her heel and caught her first glance of the soaring white Opera Garnier, home to the Garnier Ballet, with its sweeping colonnaded front and gleaming gold statues ranged along the roofline.

"I always forget how beautiful it is," she said as she craned her neck.

Max smiled indulgently and she gave him a dry look.

"That's the problem with you Europeans. You have so many beautiful buildings you take them for granted," she said as he led her across the street to the entrance.

"The way you Australians take your beaches for granted," he said.

She glanced at the facade again and her heart seemed to shimmy in her chest all of a sudden. A strange tension had been building inside her through the whole of their train ride. It took her a few seconds to recognize it: almost, but not quite, stage fright. She tried to shake it off, but the feeling persisted as they entered the foyer and were dazzled by the huge marble columns and elaborate gilt work.

She flashed back to the first time she'd performed here, five years ago. She'd been twenty-four, touring with the Royal Ballet out of London. It had been one of her first solo roles, and she'd sent Max tickets to see her dance. All night she had imagined him in the audience, imagined that she was dancing especially for him. She'd only found out afterward that his father had been ill and he'd been unable to make it.

She could feel him watching her and she forced a smile.

"Lots of memories," she said.

"Yes. When I was growing up, it was always my dream to dance here," he said.

A dream he'd never achieved, she knew. He started up the first flight of marble steps that would take them to the dress circle. She couldn't help but notice the tide of feminine interest that followed in his wake like a vapor trail.

No wonder.

She'd been hard put not to stare back at the apartment, either, when she'd come out of the bathroom in her rose print dress to find him waiting for her. His crisp white shirt, black velvet jacket and waistcoat and charcoal wool trousers fit him to perfection. His clear gray eyes were set off perfectly by the shadowy stubble on his jaw.

On any other man, the velvet would be a clear signal to lock up the Judy Garland collection, but on Max it looked elegant and refined and just right. Very French. Very sexy.

She stared after him for a long moment, aware that she was stalling. For some reason, she was loath to take her seat and watch this performance. Which was crazy. It was one of her favorite ballets and the production promised to be lavish and spectacular. Anna would be dancing, and the rest of the company were all highly experienced, excellent performers. She and Max were in for a treat.

So why did she feel as though she wanted to turn tail and run?

At the top of the stairs, Max stopped to glance at her. His expression was quizzical. He was wondering what the hell she was hanging around for. She made herself move.

"You okay?" he asked when she joined him.

Again she forced a smile. "Of course."

They ascended to the dress circle level and an usher guided them to their row. Max took her coat from her and folded it carefully over the back of her seat. She smoothed the skirt of her rose print dress and sat, concentrating on their ornate surroundings in the hope that her inappropriate nerves would dissipate.

They were surrounded on all sides by well-heeled Parisians and gawking tourists. The low hum of conversation filled the lush, velvet and gilt theater. She dropped her head back to admire the colorful ceiling painting by Chagall. She'd always liked it, although she knew many considered it sacrilege that a painter had been allowed to decorate such a historical theater with a quintessentially modern piece.

The sharp notes of the violinists readying their instruments made her start in her seat. The performance was about to begin.

Her hands found the arms of her chair. She gripped them hard as the lights dimmed. She could feel Max watching her, puzzled by her stiff posture and obvious tension. She knew she should reassure him, but the words stuck in her throat.

The orchestra launched the prelude, the violins leaping above the deeper notes of the bass and brass. The curtain trembled, then rose. She imagined the dancers poised in the wings, ready to perform.

Then, suddenly, the first dancers exploded onto the stage in a flurry of movement, leaping across the space in gravity-defying *grand jetés.* Two men and two women, dancing in perfect time, dressed in lavish, traditional costumes.

It was beautiful, compelling, stirring.

Maddy slid to the edge of her seat, eyes glued to the stage

as she followed their every move. She saw the precision of their turns, the power of their leaps, the practiced skill in their lifts and pirouettes. She held her breath for them, tensed her muscles for them.

Then the soloists came on, one man, one woman.

Her eyes filled with tears as she tracked the graceful power of their dancing. The female lead spun and her partner caught her; she fled and he pursued; he jumped, she soared after him.

The audience watched, rapt, held in thrall by their skill.

And suddenly, in a rush of blinding clarity, she knew.

She couldn't do this anymore.

Andrew and Dr. Hanson had been right. Her body was old, not up to the sort of effort she saw on the stage before her. In her heart of hearts, she'd known it for some time.

She just hadn't been ready to face it.

She would never dance professionally again.

7

MAX STIFFENED with shock as Maddy suddenly shot to her feet. He could see tears in her eyes. She pressed a hand to her mouth. Then she began pushing her way past the people seated beside her until she gained the aisle.

"Maddy!" he called after her, but she broke into a run as she raced for the exit.

The people sitting around them stirred, annoyed by the interruption. Max scooped up Maddy's coat and handbag and excused his way to the aisle. By the time he'd gained the dress circle landing, Maddy was halfway down the stairs to the foyer. He took off after her, barreling out into the Paris night.

He stood panting on the steps, scanning the crowds of tourists. He had no idea what was wrong, but he'd felt the tension vibrating through her the moment they stepped out of the Metro station. That she was profoundly distressed he had no doubt.

He caught sight of her at last, standing to the left of the entrance. Her arms were wrapped around her torso, her head was bowed. As he moved closer he saw that she was sobbing, her body racked with emotion.

"Maddy," he said, pulling her into his arms. He found the back of her head with his hand and pressed her close to his chest.

"I can't...I can't," she sobbed. She was quivering, her whole body shaking. "Not anymore. It's over. It's all gone."

He ran a soothing hand down her back.

"Maddy, what happened in there?" he asked.

She leaned back from him so she could look into his face.

"They're so good. And I could see how hard it was, how unforgiving and demanding. And I realized I can't do that anymore, Max. I don't have it in me. I want it so badly, I need it, but my body has let me down. They were right. It's over for me." Her words were rushed, almost garbled. But he understood.

Her cheeks were smudged with mascara, her mouth twisted with misery. He'd never seen a sadder, more tragic sight in his life.

"You don't know that, Maddy," he said, desperate to reassure her.

She closed her eyes. "No, Max. It's over," she said with heavy finality.

Her shoulders started to shudder, and he embraced her again.

She was inconsolable, devastated. He saw a cab dropping off some late theatergoers and raised an urgent hand. A moment later he was bundling Maddy inside and holding her in his arms as she cried all the way home. It was only ten minutes, but it felt like a lifetime.

Once they hit his apartment he led her to the couch and sat with her in his lap. She curled up against him and wept out her grief.

By the time she began to calm down, his jacket was soaked through. Slowly her tears turned to sniffs, and finally to hiccups. He leaned forward to pluck a handful of tissues from the box on the coffee table, pressing them into her hand.

"Thank you," she whispered.

"Maddy. It's going to be okay."

She was silent, and he tightened his embrace.

"I mean it. We'll work something out. We'll find you some other way to get in to see Dr. Kooperman, whatever it takes. And you've still got Dr. Rambeau to see this coming week."

She shook her head.

"No, Max. There's no point. I think I've known it for a long time. Ever since I was so slow to recover after my knee reconstruction. My body isn't up to dancing professionally anymore. I'm not up to being a prima. It's over."

"You don't know that until you've had more tests, seen more specialists," he said, refusing to let her give up on her dream. He knew what it was like to stop being a dancer. He wouldn't wish the pain of separation and the loss of passion on anyone. Especially not Maddy.

"Everyone has to retire sometime," she said quietly.

He frowned, wanting to argue, to convince her not to give up. But what she'd said was true. She was twenty-nine. The average retirement age for ballet dancers was thirty, thirty-one, tops. A few innovative ballet companies were taking on older dancers, women who'd had children then come back. But the reality was that ballet demanded an enormous amount from its practitioners. It consumed their bodies then abandoned them when they still had the bulk of their lives left to live.

He realized suddenly that he had never seriously considered the idea that Maddy might not succeed in her battle to be reinstated to her former role with the Sydney Dance Company. He'd been worried for her, certainly, but he'd been unable to conceive of a time when Maddy would not dance. It was so much an essential part of her—Maddy was a ballet dancer. She was only ever fully alive when she was *en pointe,* on stage, performing for an audience.

He knew exactly how much she had sacrificed to her vocation. Her distant, detached relationship with her mother, the result of Maddy having left home when she was fourteen to travel interstate to train at the Australian Ballet Academy. The trail of ruined relationships. The lack of any life outside her career. Maddy had given dance everything. Her life, in fact. And now she was about to discover what was left over for herself.

They were both silent a long time. Finally, Maddy began to talk.

"I can still remember my first ballet class. I bugged my mom for months before she took me. I was a year younger than anyone else, younger than they normally accepted into the class, but I'd seen Anna Pavlova dancing on television and I wanted to be her so badly that I harangued my mom night and day. That first class, Madame took us through the positions. The other girls had trouble with their turnout, with pointing their toes, with their arms. But it all seemed so natural to me. It felt like home."

He smiled, circling his hand on her back.

"I used to pretend to my friends that I was going to soccer practice and then sneak off to my dance classes," he said. "My *maman* was embarrassed, I think. I'm sure she thought it was the first sign I was gay. But *Père* told me that he had danced a little when he was young, and he always regretted letting his friends' opinions matter more than what he wanted."

"Thank God he did, because you were a beautiful dancer, Max."

He pressed a kiss into her hair.

"And you were a star, Maddy. You dazzled. You lived the dream."

"Yes."

He could hear the grief in her voice again.

"Do you know what's crazy?" she asked after a while. "People are always advising dancers to plan for the future, to save their money or study part-time or something. I never did any of those things because I could never bear to think beyond the end of my career. I mean, I've got some money saved, but I have no idea what comes next. No idea."

"Something will come," he said. "You're smart, disciplined, hardworking. Whatever you put your hand to you'll succeed in."

He could feel her smile against his chest.

"My own personal cheer squad."

"Simply telling it like it is. Just because you can't dance anymore doesn't mean your life is over, Maddy."

"I know that's true. I do. But right now, when I try to project into the future, all I get is…nothing. Emptiness."

He could hear the fear and uncertainty in her voice. At least when he had walked away from his career, he'd walked away for a reason—caring for his father. Even in his darkest moments of self-pity and regret he'd known that he was doing something worthwhile.

"You don't have to make any decisions straightaway. Take some time out. Let yourself get used to the idea before you start making any plans," he said.

"Yes."

She lifted her head and met his gaze.

"I'm sorry about *The Nutcracker*," she said.

He shrugged to show how irrelevant it was.

"I could have at least saved freaking out till the end of the performance instead of the beginning," she said.

"Maddy. Forget it, okay?"

Her gaze dropped from his eyes to his mouth then flicked back to his eyes again.

"Have I ever told what a good man you are?" she asked. "You've never let me down. I bet you've never let your sister down or your father, either."

She pressed a kiss to his mouth.

"Thank you. Thank you for always being there," she said.

She hesitated a second, then leaned close to kiss him again. This time her lips lingered a fraction longer.

He could feel himself growing hard and he willed his body to calmness. The last thing Maddy needed right now was the knowledge that while she was seeking comfort, he was getting horny.

Then Maddy kissed him a third time and he felt the distinct wet roughness of her tongue sliding across his upper lip. Desire thumped low in his belly and his fingers curled into her back instinctively.

He pulled away.

"I don't think that's such a great idea, do you?"

Her eyes were heavy-lidded and smoky with need as she tried to kiss him a fourth time. He held back, refusing the temptation.

"Just for tonight, Max. I don't want to be alone. I don't want to think or feel," she pleaded.

He hesitated. She closed the distance between them and he felt the tip of her tongue trace his lower lip.

She tasted of tears and need, and he was only human. He opened his mouth and her tongue swept inside, sliding along his own sensuously. As soon as he had one taste he wanted a whole lot more and he clamped his hand to the back of her neck and angled his mouth over hers.

She murmured her approval, her body straining toward his. His free hand slid down her shoulder and onto her breast. Her nipples were already hard and she arched into his hand.

His erection pulsed against her backside, eager to get in on the action. He flicked his thumb over her nipple again and again. She sucked hard on his tongue and dug her hands into his back, pulling him close. Then suddenly she was pushing him away and shifting in his lap so that she was straddling him as she reached for his fly.

Her hands were shaking, her breath coming fast. He tugged the straps of her dress down as she slid his zipper open. Her small, pert breasts fell free of her dress as he pushed it down and cupped her in his hands. Her hand snaked into his boxer-briefs and he closed his eyes as she gripped him.

He needed to taste her skin. With one hand behind her back, he urged her close and ducked his head to take a nipple in his mouth. She gasped, her body shuddering. He bit her gently then sucked hard. She groaned and started to pant.

"I need you, Max," she breathed.

Her body arched forward as she rose up on her knees, and then her hands were guiding him into wet heat. The realization that she must have simply pushed her underwear to one side hit him even as she slid down onto his length, taking all of him at once.

"Maddy," he groaned as she gripped him tight.

She started to ride him, her hips sinuous, one hand locked on his shoulder as she drove herself down to the hilt of him then slid up again. Her eyes were closed, her teeth sunk into her bottom lip, her face straining with need as she sought oblivion.

He felt himself starting to lose it. She was so wet and hot, so greedy for it. He'd never been with a woman who was so honest about her own needs. It was the biggest damned turn-on in the world.

He ducked his head to her breasts again, laving them with the flat of his tongue. His hands gripped her hips and he pumped into her, grinding himself against her.

He felt her tighten around him. His own body tensed as his climax thundered toward him. She threw back her head. He felt her begin to pulse around him, her body milking his. And then he lost it, his orgasm hitting him like a wall. He thrust into her one last time, his fingers tightening on her hips, his teeth bared in a grimace of pleasurable pain.

As desire faded, reality crept in. Once again things had gotten out of control between them.

He should have stopped her. Should have been strong enough to resist temptation. But it was hard to feel sincere regret when he was still inside her and his hands still on her warm skin.

She opened her eyes and stared at him. She surprised him for the second time that night by pressing a kiss to his chin.

"No regrets. Not yet," she said firmly.

He wasn't sure if she was issuing an order or giving him an emotional weather report.

His gaze swept over her body, taking in the rosy color across her breasts, her still-aroused nipples, the rapid rise and fall of her chest. Her skirt was bunched around her thighs and he badly want to lift it to see where they were joined.

Before he could act on the impulse, Maddy shifted, rising off him. Sliding free of her tight heat felt like too great a loss and he grabbed her hips before she could move farther.

"Where are you going?" he asked.

She frowned, confused.

"I'm not done with you yet," he said.

He'd surprised her. About time.

He watched as her pupils expanded to fill her irises.

"What did you have in mind?" she asked. He could see a pulse beating in her neck.

"Stuff," he said with a slow smile.

She blinked. Then her gaze dropped to his groin where he was already growing hard again.

"Oh."

"You wanted to forget," he reminded her.

She licked her lips. "Yes."

He stood on a surge of strength, taking her with him. In two strides he was at the stairs to the sleeping platform. She wrapped an arm around his neck as he ascended to the bedroom.

"Take your dress off," he said as he set her on her feet.

She hesitated for a moment, then her hands reached for her zipper. He watched as her dress fell to the ground in a rustle of silk, leaving her standing in nothing but a pair of lacy white panties.

"Get rid of these," he said, sliding his thumb inside the side elastic and letting it snap back against her skin.

She swallowed. The look she flashed him was full of anticipation and desire. She pushed her panties down her legs and stepped out of them.

"Why aren't you undressing?" she asked.

"Lie down, and lift your hips," he said, ignoring her question.

Again she hesitated for a few seconds before doing as he'd said. He slid a pillow beneath her hips.

"Now spread your legs for me, Maddy," he said, his voice low with need.

She sucked in a breath, her gaze meeting his across her prone body. Slowly, she let her thighs drop open. He let his gaze trail over her body—the straining peaks of her breasts, the taut plane of her flat, muscled belly, then finally to where she was wet with need for him.

She was pretty and pink and plump and so much more desirable than he'd ever imagined.

"Get comfortable," he said.

And then he went down.

MADDY CLOSED HER EYES as Max's dark head neared the heart of her. Suddenly she realized that she wanted to see him do this, wanted to watch him savor her.

It should have been a shocking thought: Max, her friend, about to go down on her. Instead, a deep, primitive thrill rippled through her and she grew even wetter and hotter with need.

Her eyes snapped open as she felt his breath warm on her inner thighs, then she felt the first wet, rough rasp of his tongue against her. Her whole body shuddered and her hips jerked involuntarily. He gave a murmur of approval and used his hands to explore her intimate folds while he teased her with his tongue.

Her head fell to the pillow. She was liquid with desire, her blood as thick and sticky as toffee. She groaned deep in the back of her throat as Max opened his mouth over her and kissed her passionately, his tongue firm and fast.

His hands caressed the tender skin of her inner thighs,

soothing, kneading. She slid her hands into his hair and hung on for dear life.

He began to circle her inner lips with one deft finger, gliding through her slick desire, driving her crazy. She had to grab at the sheets then, her hands fisting in the fabric, desperate for something to anchor her in a sea of sensation.

He slid a finger inside her at last and she clenched around him hungrily.

"Yes," she murmured. "Please."

He used his free hand to spread her wide, exposing her utterly as he feasted on her. Her body bowed with desire as he slid his finger in and out of her, his tongue teasing her all the while.

It was too much. He was too much. Her climax hit her, vibrating through her body in shuddering waves. The last tremor had barely left her body before Max slid inside her, his thick heat stretching her in the best possible way.

She sighed as he began to pump into her.

He supported his weight on one arm as his free hand roamed her body, caressing her neck and her shoulders before finally claiming her breasts. His eyes were dilated with desire, his face hard with tension as he drove himself into her. She stared at him, amazed at his beauty, amazed that she had spent so many years not wanting him. How was that possible when her whole body was on fire for him?

He squeezed her nipples, then soothed them in the palm of his hand. She felt the tension growing in his body as he slid both hands beneath her, cupping her backside as he thrust into her again and again.

He felt so good, so hard, so right inside her. For the third time that night, desire coiled in her belly. She gripped his hips with one hand and slid the other onto his hard butt, glorying in the flexing of his muscles as he rode her.

"Maddy," he groaned.

She tilted her hips and gave him everything she had. He shifted higher, his hard shaft pressing where she needed him most.

She lost it, hands clutching at him, gasping for air, her world reduced to the warm, throbbing place where their two bodies became one.

He shuddered, his body hard with tension, his hands clenching her backside almost painfully. He pumped into her one last time, then pressed his face into her neck as he came in a hot rush.

He collapsed on top of her, his breathing harsh. She stared at the ceiling, stunned by the intensity of what had just taken place.

After a while he withdrew and rolled onto his back. They lay side by side, sweat cooling on their bodies, the smell of sex surrounding them as their heart rates gradually slowed.

She hadn't meant to kiss him. She'd meant to thank him, to somehow express the enormous gratitude she felt for his comfort, patience and understanding. Then she'd pressed her lips to his and smelled his skin, tasted him and instantly wanted more. And, like always, he hadn't denied her.

She turned her head so she could look at him. God, he was so beautiful. She'd seen plenty of naked men in her time, but Max's body was something special. Those big, strong thighs. That hard ass. His powerful shoulders and ripped belly.

She closed her eyes, unsure what to say or do. Unsure where this left them now that they'd once again crossed the line.

A warm knee nudged her.

"Hey. Wake up, sleepyhead."

She opened her eyes. He was watching her, his eyes hooded.

"You're not allowed to sleep yet," he said.

She stared at him, unable to believe that he wanted more when they'd just consumed each other. Her gaze dropped to his thighs where he was growing harder by the second.

Unbelievable.

"You *are* T-Rex," she said without thinking. "Insatiable."

"Maybe it depends what's on offer," he said, his French accent very pronounced.

He rolled toward her, his hand finding her breast as he leaned close to kiss her. Warmth cascaded through her body as his tongue stroked hers.

There was no time for regret, she realized. Not tonight. This wasn't over, not by a long shot.

MAX WOKE TO FIND HIMSELF tangled in Maddy's hair. She lay curled away from him on her side.

He couldn't get enough of her. He'd made love to her all night, like a man possessed. He'd brought her to climax again and again, and always she'd met him, matching need for need, passion for passion.

She'd asked him to make her forget. He figured he'd fulfilled his part of the bargain, and then some.

He disentangled himself and slid to the edge of the bed, feeling the full weight of what lay in store for him today. Another speech about regret and friendship from Maddy, no doubt. And, more than likely, her departure. Now that she had faced the reality of her retirement, there was nothing to keep her here. She'd want to go home, back to her apartment and her friends and her life.

He glanced over his shoulder, his eyes tracing the curves of her body. She was so beautiful, so compelling. How was he ever going to forget her?

He closed his eyes and let his shoulders drop. The old, familiar ache tightened his chest. Stupid to fall for the same unattainable woman twice in one lifetime. But it was done, and only time would undo it.

"Good morning."

Her voice sounded husky, deeper than usual. He glanced across in time to see her pulling the sheet up to cover her breasts.

The contrast to the easy, erotic intimacy of last night was profound. Just in case he had any doubts about where he stood, her instinctive gesture told him everything he needed to know.

"How are you doing?" he asked.

She was still his friend, after all, and last night had been a watershed in her life.

She shrugged a shoulder.

"I'm not sure. I feel like I'm waiting for something else to happen. The other shoe to drop."

"Yeah. But it will get better. You'll work it out." He took a deep breath. "I guess you'll be heading home soon, then?"

There was a short pause before she answered.

"I guess so. There's nothing keeping me here anymore, after all."

Was it his imagination, or was there a slight question in her tone? He studied her, but her expression was unreadable.

Grasping at straws, man. Have a little dignity.

He reached for his boxer-briefs, lying discarded on the floor. He didn't need to look to know she glanced away when he stood and pulled them on.

The joys of the morning after.

"I'm going to grab a shower," he said.

That would give her time to pull herself together, something she clearly wasn't comfortable doing while he was around.

"Sure."

He headed down the stairs, his shoulders rigid with tension. Suddenly the thought of her going, of her not filling his space with the sound of her voice and her flowery perfume seemed like a really great idea.

He shut the bathroom door with too much force. What he really wanted to do was kick it, or punch a hole in something.

She'd offered him a taste of what he wanted, and he was going to have to live off the memory for the rest of his life.

Meanwhile, she would walk away having found comfort or indulged her curiosity or whatever the hell she'd been doing last night and the other night at the Latin club.

"Putain de merde!" he swore harshly, turning away from the mirror so he wouldn't have to look at his own sorry face.

He turned on the shower full force, welcoming the bombardment as he stepped beneath the water. He turned his face into the flow, then reached for the soap to wash her scent from his skin.

The screech of the shower curtain being yanked open filled the bathroom. Startled, he turned to find Maddy standing there wearing nothing but his shirt from the night before, the tails flapping against her bare legs, her hands planted squarely on her hips.

"I just want to know one thing," she said, her chin thrust out. "Did you sleep with me last night because you felt sorry for me and you were playing knight in shining armor again?"

"I could ask you the same thing."

"What's that supposed to mean?"

"We've been friends for years, and suddenly out of nowhere sex has become part of the equation. Why have the rules suddenly changed, Maddy?"

She opened her mouth, then closed it without saying anything.

"I asked you first," she said.

He stared at her.

"You kissed me," he reminded her. "Both times."

Her gaze slid over his shoulder and she shuffled from one foot to the other. The silence stretched between them.

She didn't want to say it, he realized. Didn't want to tell him she'd had an itch and he'd scratched it, that any handy man would have done.

"Fine," he said, reaching for the shower curtain, ready to shut her out.

"I saw you," she said in a rush.

He froze.

"That day when Charlotte called having problems with the babysitter. I knocked on the bathroom door to let you know she needed to speak to you, but you didn't answer. So I opened the door to tell you. And you were...you had your hands full. Really full," she said meaningfully.

Shit.

He closed his eyes as a wave of fiery heat rushed up the back of his neck and into his face. Even as a teenager he'd never been busted taking care of business. That Maddy had caught him red-handed—while he'd been fantasizing about her—was as bad as it could get.

"It was the sexiest, hottest damn thing I've ever seen in my life, Max."

For a second he thought he'd imagined her words. He opened his eyes and stared at her. She was the one blushing now, but her gaze was unwavering.

"I never let myself think about you like that. Ever. I valued you as my friend too much. But seeing you naked and hard...I couldn't get it out of my head," she said.

He blinked. Maddy was hot for him. Finally, after all these years, she was hot for him.

Her hands were twisting in the fabric of his shirt, and one foot rubbed the other self-consciously as the silence stretched.

It had cost her to confess what she'd seen. He felt he owed her the same honesty.

"I've always been attracted to you," he said boldly.

Her gaze flicked up, locked with his.

"What?"

"I've always wanted you. From the moment I first met you."

Her eyes widened.

"That day in the shower I was thinking about you. Imagining you were in here with me. Imagining I was inside you, touching you."

For a moment they stared at each other.

"This changes everything," she said. She sounded dazed.

"Yes," he agreed. "Come here."

She took a step closer and he hauled her the rest of the way into the stall, shirt and all. In seconds the fabric was plastered to her body, her nipples showing darkly through.

He backed her against the wall and pressed his body to hers. Then he lowered his head and kissed her, tracing her lips with his tongue before dipping inside her mouth to taste her properly. She slid her arms around his neck and wound a leg around his thigh. Her hips moved against his in a sinuous demand.

"Stay," he said when he broke their kiss.

"For how long?" she asked, a frown forming.

"A week, two weeks. A month. Does it matter?"

He wanted to say a lot more, but he wasn't a fool. Well, not a complete fool, anyway.

She searched his face. He slid a hand down her belly and between her thighs. It was cheating, and he knew it, but—

She quivered in his arms as his fingers slid into her slick heat.

"Yes," she breathed. "Yes."

It wasn't a promise. It certainly wasn't a commitment but it would do. For the time being, anyway.

8

THREE WEEKS LATER, Maddy frowned at the front page of *Le Monde* as she stood at the kitchen table, trying to translate the main story.

"What does *méchant* mean again?" she asked.

Max was at his workbench, adding some shading to his latest sketch.

"A big cigar. Or, depending on the context, a cruel man."

"So helpful. Not," she muttered under her breath.

"You'll get the hang of it," he said confidently.

Maddy was not so sure. She'd learned all the ballet technique phrases in French because she'd been passionate about her craft, and she'd picked up enough menu and incidental French to get by over the years. But actually remembering and understanding the grammar and syntax of another language seemed like a Herculean task, especially when she had no idea how to conjugate a verb in her own language, let alone a new one.

"I learned English when I was a kid," Max reminded her as he crossed to the kitchen table. "A new language is not so hard."

Warmth washed through her as he stood behind her, sliding his arms around her. For a delicious moment she savored the heat of his strong body, letting her weight rest back against him.

Three weeks of him, of this, and she still couldn't get enough. Three weeks, and she couldn't remember what it was like to not want Max, to not crave his touch. How had she ever looked at him as only a friend?

"That's different. Your mind was young and nimble. Mine is nearly thirty and stiff and arthritic," she said, only half joking.

Max laughed, the sound vibrating through her body. She felt the brush of his fingers as he pushed her hair out of the way to bare her neck. Then he kissed her, his tongue moving in lazy circles against the tender skin behind her ear.

"Mmmm." She'd been modeling for him and was wearing one of his old T-shirts and nothing else. She felt his erection pressing against her backside through the thin fabric.

"It's a wonder you ever get any work done," she said, rubbing herself against him shamelessly.

"I know. I consider it a miracle. Maybe I should give Yvette a call again."

He'd chosen to use Maddy instead of Yvette for the rest of his sketch studies. Every day Maddy modeled, and every day their sessions inevitably turned into lovemaking. Sometimes Max took her when she first disrobed, his eyes hard with desire as he walked toward her. Other days, like today, he waited until he'd captured the poses he wanted before giving in to the need they both felt.

She smiled with anticipation as one of his hands slid inside the baggy neckline of the T-shirt seeking her breasts. The other moved down her body to cup her backside.

His hands massaged her and she closed her eyes.

He knew exactly what to do to make her wild.

She moaned as he dipped his fingers between her thighs, widening her stance to invite him in. Delicate, teasing, he delved into her intimate folds.

She held her breath as he slid a finger inside her, then another.

Instantly she was on fire, her heart racing, her body clamoring for him.

"Max." She reached behind her, finding the stud on his jeans and popping it open.

In seconds he was free of his underwear, his erection rubbing against the lower curve of her backside. She leaned forward, hands stretched before her on the table, back arched, butt high, offering herself to him. He didn't need to be asked twice. He slid home in one smooth thrust.

"Maddy," he groaned.

She tilted her hips, encouraging him to move. He obliged and within seconds they were both gasping, their bodies tense with approaching orgasm.

He curled his hands into her hips and pumped into her hard and fast. She quivered, her head dropping forward bonelessly as she came, her inner muscles trembling around him. His own orgasm followed hard on the heels of hers and she felt him shudder as it gripped him.

She collapsed flat onto the table, the smell of fresh newsprint strong in her nostrils. Opening an eye, she saw she was sprawled across *Le Monde*.

"What's so funny?" Max asked.

"Maybe I've been going about learning French the wrong way," she said.

He laughed. "I can think of worse ways to learn a language. Maybe I will whisper it to you while we make love. Perhaps that will help your recall."

The thought of Max speaking soft French words in her ear while he rode her sent a shiver up her spine.

"You like that idea, do you?" he asked.

She could feel him growing hard inside her again.

She'd never had a lover like him. Insatiable. Knowing. Tender and passionate. Earthy and imaginative. It was possible he'd ruined her for any other man.

The thought made her stomach dip. One day—probably

soon if her track record was anything to go by—this fling with Max would be over and she would be forced to stop basking in the here and now and think about the future. About a life without dancing, and a life without Max.

"*J'aime te faire l'amour,* Maddy," Max murmured as he flexed his hips.

She felt the slow, delicious slide as he stroked into her. She closed her eyes and concentrated fiercely on how good it was, how good they were. As always, everything else slipped away. The future could wait another day.

"*Tu te sentez si serrée at chaude.*"

She grasped the edge of the table as one of Max's hands slid around her rib cage to find her breasts.

"*Quand je suis a l'interieur de toi—*"

They both tensed as a knock sounded at the door.

Max swore. "Perfect timing," he said with heavy irony.

"It's Charlotte," she said, suddenly remembering. "She mentioned she was going to drop by this morning."

"Of course it's Charlotte. It's been a whole day since we saw her last," he said.

She laughed, then gave a little gasp of loss as he withdrew from her.

"Blame my sister. I plan to," he said.

His obvious frustration was flattering and funny.

Charlotte knocked again, longer and louder this time.

"For Pete's sake, stop jumping each other and answer the door," she called.

Maddy reached out to tag Max's arm. "You're it," she said, taking off at speed for the bathroom.

"Hey!"

"Tell her I won't be a moment," she called over her shoulder as she shut the bathroom door.

She could hear Max laughing ruefully behind her. She had

a smile on her face, too, as she hastily pulled on underwear, a black turtleneck and jeans. She secured her hair in a low bun on the back of her neck and decided she was presentable.

"Let me guess. You were busy 'working,'" Charlotte was saying as Maddy joined them.

"Something like that."

Max was making coffee and Charlotte stabbed a sisterly finger into his chest.

"I don't know what's worse—worrying about you being single or worrying about you and Maddy wearing each other out."

Max laughed. "You'll be the first person I call from the hospital."

"How delightful for me," Charlotte said.

She caught sight of Maddy and her face lit up.

"Maddy!" She drew Maddy into a hug, kissing both her cheeks warmly.

After a rocky start, she and Charlotte had decided they liked each other. Maddy had had several more dancing sessions with Eloise, and Charlotte was warmly grateful for the pleasure her daughter found in the experience. Underneath all the stress and tiredness of managing two children on her own, Max's sister was as charming as Max himself, and Maddy had quickly discovered she liked having a female friend who discussed more than the freshest gossip from the ballet world or the effectiveness of the latest diuretic tablet or corn pads.

As Charlotte began to regale them with an update on Richard's search for a new job, Maddy felt the weight of Max's stare. She glanced over, and sure enough he was watching her, one hip propped against the kitchen counter, arms crossed over his chest. He looked very serious—brooding, almost. As soon as she made eye contact with him he smiled and the moment of intensity was gone, leaving her wondering if she'd imagined it.

"I can't believe I'm going to voluntarily subject myself to

this, but tell me what you two are up to this afternoon," Charlotte said, crossing her legs and raising an eyebrow in inquiry.

Over the past weeks, Maddy and Max had developed a routine of sorts. Most mornings she sat for him, then he worked on his sketches and other projects until midafternoon. After that he took her out into the city, showing her his Paris. So far they had toured Père Lachaise, explored the tangled streets of Montmartre, visited the Picasso museum and wound their way through the city via the secret covered corridors that made it possible for a pedestrian to walk under cover from Montmartre all the way across the city to the Palais Royal.

She didn't kid herself that their excursions were for any other reason than to entertain and distract her from her ever-circling thoughts. Max shared a bed with her—he knew she woke in the night sometimes, grief welling up inside her for the life she used to live. She never let herself cry, because it never made her feel any better. Still she couldn't stop herself from remembering and regretting and mourning.

Pointless. A huge waste of time. But she couldn't stop it. She'd spent almost her whole life wanting to be a ballerina, striving, enduring—and now it was all over. It was going to take some time to adjust. She kept thinking that if only she had known, consciously, that this was going to happen, she could have savored her last season, stored up memories, made each moment on stage count. But she hadn't. And she couldn't go back and change anything. It was what it was.

Maddy looked to Max. "We haven't decided yet."

"I was thinking the Rodin museum," he said.

"I find it hard to believe that there won't be a picnic associated with this expedition," Charlotte said archly. "Or at least a visit to a bonbon shop or a patisserie."

Maddy laughed. "Max, you see how predictable we are?"

"I can live with it," he said.

"You're going to make me fat."

He loved feeding her all the things she'd denied herself for so many years. Chocolates. Éclairs. Macaroons. She'd nearly cried when she tasted her first passion fruit and chocolate macaroon from Pierre Hermé in St. Germain last week. Max had bought one for her every day since.

Charlotte stood and collected her handbag.

"Before I forget—Richard wants to go back to Côte d'Azur again this summer, and it looks as though we can get the same house," she said to Max. "What about you? Do you have plans to go away?"

"Not yet," Max said.

Maddy knew that the city basically shut down for the month of August as Parisians headed for the coast for their summer holidays. Charlotte had already told her that good holiday houses were as scarce as hens' teeth, so it didn't surprise Maddy that she was planning ahead.

"You and Maddy should come with us. There's a private apartment attached to the back of the house—it would be perfect for you two," Charlotte said.

Maddy looked at Max, not sure how to handle the question. August was months away. She didn't even know if she would be here next week. More importantly, she didn't know if Max wanted her to be here, either. It was one thing to have great sex, as often as possible, but it was another thing entirely to start making plans together.

"I don't think so," he said. "But thanks for thinking of us."

Charlotte started to say more then shrugged. "Fine. But if you change your mind, the offer is still there."

She kissed them both goodbye then left, letting in a blast of chilly air before the door closed behind her.

Maddy found herself focusing on the hem of her sweater, fiddling with a stray thread there rather than risking eye contact with Max. She was hurt by Max's easy rejection of his sister's offer. Was he so certain she would be gone from his life by summer?

Even as the thought circled her mind, Maddy kicked herself. She couldn't hang around Max's apartment, existing on the fringes of his life for six months, even if he wanted her to. She had her own life to live—whatever that might turn out to be.

"If you keep picking at that, it's going to fall apart."

She glanced up to find Max standing close to her, his gray eyes unreadable.

"I know." She released her grip on her sweater.

Something of what she'd been thinking must have shown on her face, because he cocked his head to one side as he studied her.

"You didn't want to go to Côte d'Azur, did you?" he asked lightly.

"Of course not. It's ages away. I'll probably be teaching Pilates at Bondi Beach by then," she said.

There was a small pause before he smiled. "I thought you were going to be a personal trainer."

Over the weeks, they'd made a game out of cycling through the various professions most dancers wound up in once they'd retired. So far, they'd toyed with Maddy becoming a ballet mistress, an arts administrator and a personal trainer.

"That's so last week," she said with mock disdain.

The moment of odd tension was gone as they bantered back and forth. Max helped her into her coat and she wound his scarf around his neck, ensuring he'd be well protected from the wind.

Hats and gloves on, they walked to Rue de Rivoli, stopping along the way to buy a bottle of wine, a baguette, some cheese and a bag of grapes. Max led her to what had become her favorite picnic place, the small park at the very tip of the Isle de la Cité, the home of Notre Dame. Despite the fact that the garden had been reduced to a bunch of twigs sticking out of gravel at this time of year, Maddy loved it and dragged Max to it as often as possible.

"It's a terrible cliché, coming here, you know," he told her as they sat on a bench and tore their bread into chunks. "Perhaps the most clichéd picnic venue in Paris."

"I don't care. It's close to the river. I don't know what it is about the Seine, but it makes me feel good whenever I see it," she said. She raised her face to the sun and closed her eyes, savoring the weak warmth.

"Are you homesick?" he asked quietly. "Winter in Sydney's nothing like this."

Maddy considered the question as she smeared Camembert on her bread.

"I miss the light from home, if that makes sense. It's so bright and clear in Australia. I can see why the Impressionists went crazy with all that hazy, dazy light in their paintings over here in Europe. Everything is much softer, gentler."

"I know what you mean," he said. "I have photographs from when I was living in Sydney. They're so bright they almost hurt my eyes."

She smiled, then saw he had bread crumbs caught in his scarf. For some reason, seeing him sitting there wearing his sophisticated scarf and superbly tailored coat and Italian shoes with crumbs down his front made her heart squeeze in her chest. How could a man be so devastatingly attractive yet so boyishly appealing at the same time? Suddenly she remembered something one of Max's girlfriends from long ago had once said to her. "It's not his good looks or his body or how smart he is that really gets me. It's those gray eyes of his. They always look as though they're about to laugh at me."

Maddy realized she was staring and forced herself to look away.

This is a fling, Maddy. Don't go getting ideas. Remember your track record with men.

But Max wasn't like any of the other men she'd slept with. He understood her. He knew her. They knew each other. And she no longer had to share her time between dance and the man in her life. Max could have her night and day, week in, week out. If he wanted her.

Maddy gazed out at the river. She knew what a psychologist would say she was doing—using this thing with Max to divert herself from the hole dancing had left in her life. Max distracted her with sightseeing and gastronomic indulgences, and she rounded the job off by fixating on what was happening between them, building it up into something it probably wasn't, and probably never should be.

It wasn't fair to Max that she latch onto him to stop herself from going under. He deserved a hell of a lot more than that.

Beside her, Max crumpled the empty bread wrapper into a ball.

"Come on. Art awaits," he said, standing and holding out a hand.

She let him pull her to her feet. He was an amazing man. The best. And she had to be careful not to abuse his generosity and kindness by overstaying her welcome. She had to make sure she left before the sex palled and she became a burden instead of a friend in need.

Max tucked her arm through his and led her off the island and onto the left bank. As they walked, he pointed out his favorite buildings and told her a little about their histories. Being Paris, the stories were all colorful and drenched in blood and revolution.

She let herself be wrapped in his warm charm. It was wrong to lean on him so much, but right now she wasn't quite sure how to stand on her own two feet. Soon, she would find a way to be strong again.

The Musée Rodin was in a stately old mansion with spacious, highly manicured grounds. Like so much of Paris, it was beautiful and elegant and Maddy looked around admiringly as Max bought their tickets.

He grew quiet as they walked into the first room. He stopped in front of each sculpture, no matter how small, his eyes caressing the curves and planes Rodin had created.

"This is like a church for you, isn't it?" she said quietly after they'd toured the ground floor and were climbing the stairs to the second level.

"He changed the world," he said simply. "Breathed life into sculpture again."

Finally they wound up out in the gardens, standing in front of two enormous cast bronze doors; the entire surface of them was writhing with figures, animal and beast, bursting from the surface into three dimensions. Torsos twisted, arms lifted beseechingly, legs flailed in torment. Appropriate, given the piece was titled *The Gates of Hell*.

Maddy's eyes were wide with awe as she cataloged the detail, the sheer breadth and scope of the work.

"This is…amazing," she said.

"Yes."

He turned on his heel and started up the gravel path leading deeper into the garden. She knew from consulting the map that there were no more sculptures in that direction, but she followed him anyway. At the far end was a fountain, dry at present, and he sat on its rim and stared at his loosely clasped hands.

She sat beside him, tucking her own hands into her pockets for warmth. After a few minutes, Max started talking.

"The first time I came here was with my grandfather. I bitched and moaned all the way because I wanted to ride my bike with my friends instead. But my grandfather was determined to introduce me to a bit of culture. Then I walked in the door and saw the first sculpture and I stopped dead in my tracks." He shook his head, smiling at the memory. "My heart was pounding. I wanted to close my eyes. The sculptures seemed so dynamic and powerful they scared me. My grandfather didn't say a word. He took one look at my face, then led me from room to room. I think we were here for over three hours, that first visit."

Maddy watched Max's face as he went on to talk about the art they'd seen, smiling now and then at his passion, the way he gesticulated so energetically as he tried to evoke an image or underscore his meaning.

"I'm probably boring you into a coma," he said after a while. "Blink for me. Prove to me that you're not catatonic."

She laughed. "You're not boring me. I'm learning a lot. I'm basically ignorant about almost everything in the world except for dance, you know. I didn't even know how a bronze was made until you explained it to me. I love listening to you talk about art."

He rolled his eyes and she nudged him with her elbow.

"I do! You get all French and you get this light in your eyes."

"Like a crazy man."

"Like a man who's found his passion," she said.

He shrugged self-consciously.

"I'd give anything to be like you. To have something else I loved as much as dancing," she said.

The words were out before she could edit them, and she bit her lip.

"That sounds so greedy, doesn't it? I've had all these years of dancing at the top of my game, and you didn't even get to really explore your dancing career. Now you've got a second chance to do something you love and I'm sitting here grouching about how jealous I am."

"Stop giving yourself such a hard time for being a human being, Maddy," he said.

"I just wish there was something—anything—that I wanted to do," she said.

The despair that crept up on her in the dead of the night threatened, and she curled her hands into fists inside her pockets. All her life she'd lived through her body, but now her most evocative, finely honed tool of self-expression, therapy, exercise and solace had been taken away from her.

"Come here," Max said.

He tugged on her arm until she allowed him to pull her into his lap so that she sat straddling him.

"Something will come up," he said, as he had said so many times over the past few weeks. That, and variations of *give it time, don't rush yourself*. She knew he was right. She only wished whatever it was would get a wriggle on. She needed something to hold on to, stat.

In the interim, she clung to Max as he kissed her.

Their bodies quickly grew heated beneath their coats. Max tugged off his gloves and slid his hands under her top and onto her breasts. She sighed into his mouth as he squeezed her nipples gently. Under the guise of ensuring she was warm, he opened his jacket so that she nestled inside the flaps. She swallowed with excitement when his fingers found the stud on her jeans.

"Max. We're at a museum," she whispered, even though she was slick with need.

"I can't think of a better place for it. Think of it as performance art."

She bit her lip as he pulled down her fly and slid his hand inside her panties. She felt him brush through her hair, then he was gliding into her heat.

"So wet, Maddy," he murmured, kissing her neck.

"I wonder whose fault that is?"

His clever middle finger found her and began to stroke her firmly. She clenched her thighs around his hips and gripped his shoulders. At the far end of the walkway she could see a tour group turning onto the gravel path.

"Someone's coming," she said, trying to pull his hand away.

"I know," he said.

She couldn't help but laugh.

"Not me. Real people. Tourists," she said.

She bit her lip again as he upped the pace.

"We'd better be quick then, yes?" he said.

Useless to pretend that the danger, the illicit nature of what they were doing wasn't a turn-on. Desire built inside her and she gasped as her climax hit her. Max kissed her, swallowing her small cry.

By the time the tourists arrived at the fountain, he'd buttoned her jeans again and she had her flushed face pressed against his neck.

"Don't think there won't be payback," she said when the tourists had gone. "Sleep with one eye open, because you are going down, mister."

"And that is supposed to be a punishment, Maddy?" he said, sounding very French as he laughed at her.

She tapped him on the nose with her finger.

"Mark my words—you'll get yours."

"Oooh," he said.

They stood and slowly walked back to the museum.

Max slid his arm around her shoulder and kissed the top of her head. A warm glow spread through her—and it had nothing to do with the orgasm he'd just given her. She loved that she could make him laugh, and that he'd talked to her about his art and that even after three weeks, he still seemed to desire her. She loved his tender touch and his endless patience and kindness and optimism.

As they walked past a window, Maddy caught sight of their reflection, saw the small, private smiles on their faces, the way they were twined around each other as though they couldn't bear to not be touching.

They looked like a couple. Lovers, in the full meaning of the word.

Don't turn this into something it isn't, she warned herself. *Don't mix great sex with your grief and gratitude and his kindness and come up with something that doesn't exist.*

She forced herself to release Max on the pretext of adjusting her scarf. Then she forced herself to shove her hands into her pockets to resist the lure of putting her arm around him again.

It seemed like an awfully long walk home.

A WEEK LATER, Max lay in bed, his arms behind his head. He could hear Maddy puttering around in the kitchen below, and he smiled to himself.

"How are you doing?" he called out.

"Fine. Stay there," she warned.

She'd promised him pancakes for breakfast when she'd rolled out of bed twenty minutes earlier.

"And not those thin, ungenerous French excuses for pancakes, either," she'd said on her way down the stairs.

Charlotte had made a valiant attempt to interest Maddy in haute cuisine, but finally they had both agreed that simpler fare was more Maddy's thing. So far, she had mastered scrambled eggs, pancakes and a chicken and vegetable soup.

He made a bet with himself over what would go wrong this time. Something always did. Maddy had a knack for creating drama in the kitchen.

He was about to head downstairs to ensure he had a ringside seat when the phone rang.

"I'll get it," he called, reaching across the bed to take the call.

"Bonjour," he said into the phone.

There was a slight pause before someone spoke.

"Ah, *bonjour.* Ah, *non parle français, pardon moi.* My name is Perry Galbraith. I'm looking for Madeline Green." Perry's accent was broad and flat, as Australian as they came.

"Sure. I'll get her," Max said.

He frowned as he levered himself up off the bed.

Who the hell was Perry? And why was he calling Maddy in France?

"Maddy. It's for you. Some guy from home called Perry Galbraith," he said.

There was a surprised silence.

"Perry? I hope everything's all right."

She climbed the stairs to take the call. He resisted the urge to demand more information. Because he desperately wanted to eavesdrop on their conversation, he pulled on some clothes and forced himself to walk away and give her privacy.

He'd started work on his first sculpture five days ago and progress was slow but sure. He was opening a new slab of clay in preparation for the day's work when Maddy joined him ten minutes later.

"Everything okay?" he asked.

"I think so. Perry's my neighbor. I e-mailed him and asked him to collect my mail for me. He was worried about a letter that he thought might be an overdue bill."

"Was it?"

"Yeah. I'll jump online later and take care of it. I told Perry to forward the rest of my mail onto me here. I hope that's okay?"

The tension banding his shoulders relaxed.

She wasn't going home. Not yet.

"Of course. My home is your home, Maddy, you know that," he said.

"I should have thought about my bills. I've been so disorganized. Just letting the days drift away."

Her face was very serious. He'd woken in the night to find

her lying beside him more times than he could count, stiff with anxiety as she stared into the darkness. She was worried about what to do with the rest of her life—and he didn't have any answers for her. He'd busted his ass over the past four weeks, doing his best to keep her busy and entertained and distracted. He hated seeing her sad, couldn't bear the broken, deserted look she got in her eyes sometimes.

He wiped his hands on a rag and approached her.

"It's only been four weeks," he said, putting his arms around her. "You deserve some time to get used to your new reality. You've earned it."

She pressed her cheek against his shirt.

Even as he spoke, he wondered how self-serving his advice was. How much of what he was saying was for Maddy, and how much was about keeping her close, extending their time together, building the connection between them so that she might begin to see him as more than a friend and a warm body to bump against?

Hope springs eternal.

Whoever had coined that phrase had known what he or she was talking about. Max had already had more of Maddy than he'd ever imagined he'd get. To crave more, to allow himself to imagine her as part of his life, a permanent fixture in his bed and his apartment...

It was asking for trouble, being greedy. Setting himself up for a mighty, mighty fall.

And yet he couldn't stop himself from hoping. The past four weeks had been the best of his life. Sexually, emotionally, professionally—it was all coming together. If only there wasn't the growing sense that the clock was ticking, that one day soon Maddy was going to make a decision about her future—and it wouldn't include him.

He had no idea how she felt about him. He knew she desired

him. Her body told him that every time he looked at her or touched her. One kiss, one stroke of his hand on her skin was enough to make her heavy-lidded and hungry for him.

He knew she enjoyed his company and appreciated his sense of humor. She liked his family, despite the rocky start with his sister. But she'd never said a word or done anything to give him reason to believe that what was happening between them was anything more than a new aspect to their already established relationship. They were friends—and now they were friends who slept with each other.

She pressed a kiss to his jaw and stepped away from him.

"I'm a coward," she said, pushing her hair over her shoulder. "I know I should stop treading water, but I can't quite make myself do it just yet."

Treading water.

Right.

While he was building castles in the air, Maddy was keeping her head above water.

His jaw was tight as he reached for his clay cutter and began slicing thin, uniform slabs from the block.

"I'd better get back to those pancakes," she said.

She turned away, then turned back again.

"I meant to mention—I saw in the paper that more tickets have been released for Madonna's concert next month. I saw her a long time ago in Sydney. She was so fantastic. You should definitely go if you get the chance."

He looked at her.

"Come with me," he said, sick of all the uncertainty. He'd played it safe when his sister mentioned the August holidays but the concert was mere weeks away. If Maddy couldn't commit to that, then he was kidding himself well and truly.

She looked arrested, then thoughtful. Then she frowned.

"It's more than a month away, Max."

"So?"

"That's a long time for me to hang around your neck."

He couldn't tell if she was serious or joking. Whether she was looking for an easy out or if she was genuinely concerned.

"Maybe I like having you around my neck," he said, striving to keep things light. "Maybe I think you're better than a winter scarf for keeping out the cold."

She studied him before she smiled.

"Okay, let's go. But you have to tell me the moment I start getting on your nerves," she said.

"Scout's honor," he said, holding up a random number of fingers.

Another month to look forward to. Four weeks more of Maddy.

Anything could happen.

"Very convincing. Remind me not to ever get lost in the bush with you," she said, laughing.

Her eyes were bright with amusement, and soft color warmed her cheeks. All of a sudden words were crowding his throat, demanding to be said.

Words like *I love you* and *Don't ever leave.*

Words that filled his head, swelled his chest.

He dragged his gaze away from her, forced himself to concentrate on the cool, smooth, slippery texture of the clay beneath his hands.

It's too soon, he repeated to himself for the tenth time that day. *Too soon.*

But maybe, one day, he would reach the tipping point where he risked more by staying silent than by speaking out.

9

THE NEXT MORNING, Maddy rolled over in bed and felt the coolness of empty sheets beside her. Already half-awake, she sat up with a frown and stared at the indentation Max's head had left in the pillow.

She hadn't heard him get up. She felt ridiculously cheated. Lingering between the sheets in the morning with her head on his chest, his hands moving in slow circles on her back was one of the highlights of the day. Inevitably they wound up making love—long, slow sex that seemed to last for hours.

She couldn't think of a better way to start the day.

"Max? Come back to bed and warm my feet," she hollered.

The profound silence that greeted her confirmed she was alone. She pulled on one of his T-shirts and made her way downstairs.

She found his note propped against the toaster. Her love of all bread-based products after years of self-imposed deprivation had become a running joke between them—the toaster was the one appliance he knew she'd make a beeline for on waking.

Maddy, am helping Richard shift furniture. Back after lunch.
Max.

She remembered now that Charlotte had asked Max to help

move the furniture from their spare bedroom into storage so Richard could set up his new home office, an idea his employer had agreed to try in order to avoid losing Richard's expertise.

The question was, why hadn't Max woken her? She could have helped.

She had a sudden mental image of the big bed and the even bigger chest of drawers and bookcase that furnished the guest room. Okay, probably she wouldn't have been an enormous help. But still. She could at least have stood on the sidelines and cheered and made coffee.

"Pathetic," she said, shaking her head.

Surely she could survive a few hours without Max.

She straightened her shoulders and reached for the fruit loaf that Max had left for her. After she'd munched her way through three slices, she cleaned up, washing last night's dinner dishes while she was at it, then straightened the rest of the kitchen. From there she went on to sweep and mop the floors, then put in a load of washing.

It felt good to work. To have a purpose and a goal, even a short-term one. She missed the certainty and order and purpose of her old life.

All the sightseeing and fun with Max, all the indulgences and distractions—she could tap-dance around and paper over the cracks all she liked, but the truth was there was a huge void in her life where her vocation used to be and nothing was going to fill it or make it go away.

Hard on the heels of the acknowledgment came a rush of emotion, the ache of loss rising up inside her like a flash flood, all the feelings she'd banked for the past few weeks swamping her.

Suddenly she was gasping, tears flooding her eyes, her chest aching with grief and anger and a strange kind of resentment.

She was twenty-nine. Most people her age were just starting

to hit milestones in their chosen professions, moving up the food chain, getting pay raises, buying bigger cars, bigger houses. She was washed-up. She'd peaked and crashed, and now she was going to be playing catch-up for the rest of her life, trying to make do with a career that paid the rent but didn't feed her soul.

A great wave of despair hit her and she fought back a childish desire to throw back her head and wail, "Why me?"

She pressed a hand to her chest where it hurt the most, gulping back her sadness.

The worst thing was, she didn't feel like herself anymore. She'd always been inseparable from her career. Now, she was an empty shell, a doll with her insides all scooped out. Only when she was with Max was it possible for her to feel normal and forget, because he made her laugh and aroused her and challenged her.

She was hyperventilating, in the grip of a panic attack. She snatched up her phone and pressed the first digits of Max's number.

He would come to her. Or she would go to him. It didn't matter. Once she was with him, she would be okay.

She was about to press the send button when she realized what she was doing: using Max as a security blanket.

She threw her phone onto the couch and sat beside it, her head in her hands.

She was such a mess. Her career was over, she had no idea what she wanted to do with the rest of her life, and she'd embarked on a hot, breathless love affair with one of her best friends as a bizarre form of coping mechanism.

You can't keep running. It's all going to catch up with you eventually.

Maddy sucked in big mouthfuls of air, trying to slow her frantically beating heart. Her body was filled with adrenaline, responding to ancient fight-or-flight instincts triggered by her bone-deep fear of the future and the vast sorrow inside her.

"Get a grip, Maddy. For God's sake," she muttered into her hands.

Tears had squeezed out of her eyes but she wiped them from her face and stood, shaking her hands to try to relieve the tension banding her body. She needed to do something, to get out of the apartment, out of her own head. She needed to—

She closed her eyes then as she understood what her body and soul wanted, needed, demanded. She crossed to her dance bag and pulled out her pointe slippers. She found an old leotard in the bottom of the bag.

Calm washed over her as she dressed and tied her slippers and walked to the center of Max's work space. It was still essentially empty, since he'd begun work on his first piece beside his workbench near the wall. She had room to move. Room to dance.

She didn't need any music. It was all in her head. Head bowed low, she struck a position and slowly unfurled, arms rising even as she came up *en pointe*. Eyes closed, she let the music in her head and the memories in her body guide her.

She danced. She spun. She soared. She sweated. She ached. She burned.

It was heaven and hell—the thing she was born to do, but was no longer free to pursue.

MAX ROLLED his aching shoulders as he walked into the kitchen of his sister's apartment. She was busy making sandwiches, but glanced up.

"You owe me. Big-time," she said.

He raised his eyebrows.

"Excuse me? I thought I was the one who just shifted around fifty tons of antique furniture," he said.

"I had to stand in line for half an hour for those macaroons you wanted for Maddy," Charlotte said, indicating a white-paper-wrapped parcel on the bench. "In the cold. With a bunch of desperate macaroon lovers who would have killed me to take my place if they could have got away with it."

"Maddy will be eternally grateful. I will make sure she knows that sacrifices were made to secure these macaroons," he said.

Charlotte rolled her eyes. "Don't try to charm me. It doesn't work, I'm your sister."

Still, she was smiling.

Max checked his phone messages as Charlotte slid a plate his way.

"Thank you for helping out today," she said as Richard entered the kitchen.

Thin and wiry, Richard stood a full foot and a half taller than his wife. He stopped to drop a kiss onto the crown of her head before leaning over her to snare a sandwich.

Max put his phone away. No messages from Maddy. He felt a ridiculous sense of disappointment. They'd been apart a whole three hours. Unless the apartment had caught fire, there was no reason for her to call.

Unless she missed him the way he missed her.

When he looked up, Charlotte was watching him knowingly.

"What?" he said.

"Have you told her how you feel yet?"

"Charlotte…"

"You might as well answer her," Richard said around a mouthful of sandwich. "You know what she's like. She won't let up until you've given her name, rank and serial number and the keys to Fort Knox."

He slid his arm around his wife as he spoke, and she leaned into his embrace.

"Maddy and I are fine, thanks," Max said.

"Perhaps," Charlotte said.

Max narrowed his eyes. What the hell did that mean? Had Maddy said something to her about him, about them? The two women had gone shopping together the other day. He could only imagine the interrogation his sister would have subjected Maddy to.

He forced himself to take a bite of his sandwich and chew slowly. He'd regressed to high school for a full twenty seconds there as he teetered on the brink of pumping his sister for information. It was vaguely disturbing, but so much of his thinking where Maddy was concerned was off the charts. He loved her more every day, the warmth and size and scope of it expanding never-endingly. He adored her. Worshipped her. Craved her. And his fear of losing her grew exponentially at the same time.

"I've been worried about Maddy," Charlotte said.

He frowned, all his good intentions flying out the window. "What do you mean? Has she said something?"

"No. It's just that when I'm with her, I always get the sense that she's covering. She's smiling and laughing, but I can feel the sadness inside her."

Max put down his sandwich and pushed the plate away.

"She misses dancing," he said. "But she's getting over it. Transition is a hugely difficult time for dancers. That's why there are counseling services in the U.S. and the U.K. to help dancers come to terms with life after dance, to retrain and find a different path. You've got to understand, it's not just a job Maddy has lost. She's lost her identity, her community, her routine. It's going to take time."

"You sound like a brochure," Charlotte said.

"I've been reading up on it," he admitted.

"Have you ever thought that this is probably the very worst time that you two could get together?" his sister asked.

Max frowned.

"It's true, you know it is. She's a mess. She needs you. You love her. Not exactly the best basis for a relationship."

"It's not a relationship," he forced himself to say.

"You want it to be. Don't pretend you don't."

He reached for the parcel of macaroons. "Thanks for these. I'd better get home."

Charlotte reached out a hand to stop him leaving.

"Max. I know you think I'm being an interfering cow, but I love you. I want you to be happy more than anything. I think Maddy is great, you know I do. I would love for things to work out between you."

"But?"

"But she might not be ready. She's in crisis. In mourning. Confused, anxious about the future."

"You don't think she's with me for the right reasons?" Max asked.

"I don't think she knows up from down right now. She's surviving from day to day. So just... I don't know. Take it easy."

He laughed humorlessly. "Right. Thanks. I'll try to remember that."

He decided to walk home rather than take the Metro. Buds were starting to appear on the trees lining the Seine, and there was a definite hint of warmth in the air. Winter was drawing to a close, and soon it would be spring. The tourists would flood back into the city, and the streets would be full of bikes and pedestrians.

Would Maddy be here to see it?

He wanted to pin her down so badly it hurt. He wanted to declare himself and commit himself and have her do the same, to end the doubt and uncertainty forever. Ten years he'd been waiting for Maddy. Now he had her in his bed, in his life, and he wanted to keep her there.

He stopped on the small pedestrian bridge that joined the Isle de la Cité to the Isle Saint Louis. A busker on a piano accordion played an Edith Piaf tune for the tourists as Max stared down at the rushing gray waters of the Seine.

After long moments his head came up and he turned toward home with renewed purpose.

He would tell her. He would let her know how he felt, how he'd always felt. Then it would be up to her.

A strange mix of anticipation and relief washed over him. Finally, he would know. No more doubt.

He stepped up his pace. Past the Metro stop at St. Paul, into the Jewish quarter. Past the Place des Vosges. Then he was on his street, the peeling red paint of his front door calling him like a beacon.

He balanced the parcel of macaroons on one knee as he fished for his house keys and slid them into the lock.

"Maddy, I'm back," he called as he walked into the warmth of the apartment. He glanced toward the loft, then the kitchen, then the couch, but Maddy wasn't anywhere.

"Max."

His head shot around and he saw Maddy sitting on the floor against the wall, her knees pulled up to her chest, arms wrapped around them. She was wearing her pointe slippers and a leotard, and her eyes were so filled with sadness and grief that he felt as though someone had punched him in the gut.

"Maddy," he said.

He dropped the macaroons onto the nearest table and crossed to her, falling to his knees.

Her skin was covered in gooseflesh and she was shivering. Sweat darkened the fabric of her leotard and her hair was damp. She'd been dancing, he realized. Dancing until she was dripping with sweat and exhausted.

Wordless, he wrapped her in his arms. She clung to him, buried her face in his shoulder.

"I'm sorry," she said. "I thought I was doing okay but once you were gone and I was on my own, I just…fell apart."

"You don't need to apologize to me for feeling sad, Maddy," he said, one hand stroking her hair.

"It's so big," she said quietly. "This feeling inside me, this horrible emptiness. I don't know what to do with it."

"Maybe you don't have to do anything with it. Maybe it just is."

She shivered then, pressed herself closer to him.

"What if it never goes away? What if I feel this sad for the rest of my life? Max, I'm so scared. I don't know what to do next. I know I need to pull myself together, make some decisions, but there's nothing I want to do except dance. Nothing."

She sounded utterly bereft and exhausted. Max closed his eyes and held her tight, wishing he could take away the pain for her.

"Come on, let's get you into the shower."

He helped her to her feet and led her into the bathroom, turning on the hot water and kneeling to untie her ribbons. She rested a hand on his head for balance, her fingers in his hair.

"You're so good to me, Max," she said.

She peeled off her leotard and stepped into the shower. When he started to draw the curtain across behind her, she caught his hand.

"Aren't you coming in with me?"

There was a plea in her eyes and he knew what she wanted, needed from him.

Silently he stripped and joined her. Silently he kissed her, his hands sliding onto her breasts. He kissed and caressed and teased her until she was trembling in his arms then he turned off the water and carried her to the loft where he dried her gently and made love to her until she was liquid and lax in his arms.

She fell asleep with a small smile on her lips and a hand curled around his bicep. He lay awake beside her for a long time. Then he slid out from beneath her hand, rolled out of bed and made his way quietly downstairs to his desk.

His address book was there and he picked it up and thumbed through it, thinking of his friends, of past colleagues and contacts. Picking up the phone, he called the first number.

Over the next hour he spoke to half a dozen of his old dancing friends. One was in the Netherlands, two in New York, one in Australia, one in London. He told them what he was looking for and why and for whom. Then he rejoined Maddy. She stirred in her sleep, burrowing into him. He put his arms around her and lay with her hair spread across his chest and his shoulder, the scent of her filling his senses. Closing his eyes, he inhaled deeply and savored the feel and the smell and the sound of Maddy in his arms.

MADDY WOKE LATER that afternoon to find Max standing beside the bed, a tray in hand.

"Hungry?" he asked.

She blinked and pushed the hair from her eyes. Her body felt sore, tired, and her eyes were gritty. She remembered, then, in a rush of self-consciousness.

"God. I'm so sorry. You must think I'm a fruitcake," she said.

"I've got croissants, quiche and a green salad, and a nice glass of pinot noir for you," he said, ignoring her apology.

She sat up and he lowered the tray onto her lap. Then he sat on the edge of the bed and helped himself to one of the plates he'd prepared.

She watched him, feeling acutely foolish.

She'd arrived on his doorstep out of nowhere after eight years of sporadic contact, thrown herself on his chest, cried on his shoulder, jumped his body and fallen at his feet in despair. She was like an over-the-top ballet, all high notes and melodrama.

"Maddy. Stop thinking, start eating. I swear I don't think you're a fruitcake."

"Maybe I am." She picked up her fork. "Penelope Karovska had a nervous breakdown when they retired her. Joulet became an alcoholic."

"If she wasn't one already. And you're not like either of them."

She sliced off a chunk of quiche with the edge of her fork.

"You're heartbroken," he said simply. "Something you love has been taken away from you."

She stared at the food on the end of her fork, then forced herself to put it in her mouth. Max had bought this for her. While she slept off her crazed dancing bout, he'd prepared food and come up here ready to listen and offer yet more advice and patience and wisdom.

She looked at him, her gaze taking in the charming unevenness of his dark hair, growing out from the harsh cropped style now, the elegant blades of his cheekbones, the full sensuousness of his mouth. He hadn't shaved today and his jaw was shaded with bristle. His clear gray eyes stared back at her, slightly crinkled at the corners, a question in them.

"What did I do to deserve you?" she asked quietly.

For a moment there was a flare of something in Max's eyes. Then he blinked and shrugged.

"Something really decadent," he said. "I'm hoping you'll give me a live action replay of it later."

He leered so comically that she had to laugh. She ate another piece of quiche and took a sip of her wine. He told her about his morning moving furniture with Richard, showing off his scraped shin and bruised knuckles. They laughed over Charlotte's bossiness, then he produced a white parcel with an all-too-familiar name on it.

"How did you get these?" she asked, sitting up straighter. "I thought you were working all morning."

"I have my ways."

Reverently she peeled the paper from the box. The scent of

sugar and vanilla and almonds rose up to greet her and she inhaled deeply.

"Your country truly has a great gift for doing wonderful things with flour and sugar," she said.

"Don't forget butter. We're no slouches there, either."

He picked up a macaroon and brought it to her lips.

"One bite. Tell me what it is," he said.

Her teeth crunched through crisp meringue and into a creamy fondant center. She savored the flavors on her tongue for a few seconds before swallowing.

"Easy. Vanilla and pistachio," she said smugly.

"Humph. What about this one?"

They worked their way through the box and she only got one wrong. As a reward, Max ate the last macaroon off her belly then slid lower for dessert.

As she fisted her hands in the sheets and arched beneath the teasing, enticing ministrations of his hands and mouth, she felt the last of the sadness and grief she'd experienced drift away. Not gone for good, she knew that, but gone for today. Thanks to Max. Beautiful, sexy, strong, kind, patient, funny Max.

"I want you inside me," she said as she felt her climax rising. "Now, Max, please."

She felt as though a new understanding was building inside her, keeping pace with her desire, and she welcomed him into her body with greedy need.

The familiar weight of him, the rasp of his hairy, strong chest against her breasts, the slide of his body inside hers. She wrapped her legs around his waist and held on for dear life, held on to Max, as her orgasm hit her.

He came at the same time and she bit her lip as the fierce thrust and shudder of his body in hers pushed her higher and higher.

Afterward, he rolled onto his back, taking her with him so that she sprawled across his chest. His hands stroked her hair and her back and she listened to the thundering of his heart as it slowly returned to normal.

A fierce, warm awareness spread through her, a sense of well-being and belonging. This man...she'd thought she'd known him, top to bottom, inside out when she lived with him years ago. But she had never really looked at him or understood him.

He was... She didn't have the words for it.

No, that was a lie. She had the words. She simply didn't know how to say them to him yet.

She frowned, smoothing a hand over his arm, tracing the curve of his muscles. It wasn't what she'd come to Paris to find. But it had happened anyway.

She'd fallen in love with Max.

It was both a terrifying and an exhilarating thought. All her life, she'd held off from intimacy with men because experience had taught her that intimacy always came hand in hand with demands, because she'd never found a man she'd been prepared to compromise her love of dancing for.

But dancing was no longer part of her life. Briefly she wondered if being forced into retirement had allowed her to see Max differently, allowed her to make room in her heart for something other than ballet. Then she remembered the powerful need to see Max she'd felt the day she'd been given the news her career was over. Was it possible that deep down inside she'd always known that Max was the one?

The phone rang and Max stirred beneath her.

"I'd better get that," he said.

She murmured her protest and he smiled.

"It might be important. I'm expecting a call."

She let him edge away from her then shifted onto her belly and inhaled his scent from the sheets, a foolish smile on her face.

She was in love. Possibly for the first time in her life, if the feeling in her chest was anything to go by. It literally ached with fullness, with the need to wrap her arms around him and invite him into her body and protect him and adore him and love him. She squeezed her eyes tightly shut, feeling as though she was riding a roller coaster of realization and emotion.

Max. After all these years.

She heard his feet on the stairs as he returned from taking the call. She wondered if her love was in her eyes, blazing there for him to see. She felt as though it was radiating from her body, a physical energy pouring from her like light from a lamp.

She wanted to tell him, to declare herself. And yet she was scared, because he had never said anything to her about his feelings. He had been kind. He desired her. He loved her, she had no doubt, as a friend. But was he *in love* with her? Could she really be that lucky?

She turned and propped herself up on her elbows as Max stopped at the end of the bed. He still had the phone in one hand, and she saw that he'd pulled on a pair of jeans.

"Maddy, I have some great news for you," he said.

She frowned, because her mind was totally elsewhere.

"Sorry?"

"I called around, spoke to a few old dancing buddies. Remember how you told me Liza was with the Nederlands Dans Theatre?"

Her frown deepened. "Yes."

She had a sudden horrible thought. Max hadn't bought them tickets to a performance, had he? Because she wasn't up to watching other people dance yet. Certainly not someone she had once shared a stage with. One day, she would enjoy being in the audience at a ballet again. But not yet.

"She phoned to let me know that the company is forming a new offshoot, a sort of collaborative partnership, I guess, headed by some of their senior dancers. People like you, Maddy, who've been pushed into retirement before they're ready. Liza wasn't sure on the details, but she gave me a number and I called. They're looking for experienced, skilled dancers, people other companies won't consider because of their age or injuries. The plan is to choreograph to their strengths, to perform ballets that rely more on the advanced skill and technique of the dancers instead of athleticism and flexibility. I just spoke to Gregers Roby. They'd love to meet you and talk to you about dancing with them, Maddy."

She stared at him, his words ringing in her ears.

"Dance? But I can't, Max, my knee..." she said, shaking her head.

"They would play to your strengths, Maddy. Shorter sequences, shared responsibility for leads. Whatever it takes to keep someone with your skill and talent onstage for as long as they can."

She dropped flat onto her back, staring blindly. She felt dizzy, overwhelmed. She could dance again?

She could dance again?

Hard on the heels of a burgeoning, tentative hope came the realization that Max had done this. He'd contacted his friends, asked around, found something for her. Found a way to give her what she most wanted.

Found a way to send her back into her life, her old life. Her life without him.

"Why?" she asked.

She felt the bed dip as Max sat.

"Because you're an exquisite dancer. Because they'd kill to have you," Max said.

"No. Why did you call your friends? I don't understand."

There was a short pause, as if he considered his response.

"I knew you were unhappy. I thought if maybe there was a teaching role, choreography, even dance notation available, that maybe... I know you didn't think you wanted to do any of those things, but I thought that at least you would still be a part of the dance world. You wouldn't have to give it up entirely. But Liza had heard about this new company being formed, and she made some inquiries for me."

She closed her eyes. She wasn't sure what she was feeling, whether she could dare to believe in this potential reprieve.

"They know about my knee?" she asked, in case he hadn't made it clear enough to them and they thought they'd be talking to a whole dancer. "They know about my injury?"

"Yes, of course. And they still want to talk to you."

She pressed her hands to her face, overwhelmed.

"Are you okay?" Max asked.

"I can't believe it," she said.

She sat up then and faced him.

"I don't know what to say to you. You've given me so much already. Max…you've saved my life these past few weeks. And now this…"

His expression remained serious before he smiled.

"You were born to dance, Maddy," he said.

"Yes."

She flung herself at him and held him so tightly her joints ached with the effort of it.

"Max. Thank you. Thank you," she said.

"Maddy." His arms tightened around her just as firmly.

They sat that way for a long moment, holding each other fiercely. Then a horrible thought hit her.

I'll have to leave him. I'll have to leave Max to dance.

No.

The single word resounded like a shout in her mind. No. She couldn't leave Max. She couldn't possibly walk away from these feelings.

Max's grip slackened and she sensed he was about to break their embrace. She couldn't let him go. She *wouldn't* let him go, she decided. As he tried to ease away from her, she maintained the embrace. After a few seconds, he relaxed into it again, intuiting her desire—her need—for the contact.

Quickly she made plans in her mind. The company would be based in the Netherlands somewhere, probably Amsterdam, just a short flight from Paris. She could visit Max between tours, and when she had a break from rehearsals. And he could come visit her. They could take turns. She could watch his sculptures come alive. She could still have him in her life.

Only when she'd organized her thoughts and decided she could have it all did she bring herself to release him.

"They want to see you the day after tomorrow," Max said. "I know it's late notice, but they're in the last stages of planning and your availability was a bit of a wild card for them."

She widened her eyes in shock, a thousand practical considerations hitting her like an avalanche.

"My God. I'll need to book a flight. Shit, I don't even have a suitcase. What am I talking about? I came here with barely anything. I've got nothing to put in a suitcase." She laughed, feeling a little dizzy with the newness of it all.

He watched her, his gaze intent.

"Happy, Maddy?" he asked. "This is what you wanted, isn't it?"

She thought of what lay ahead—the opportunity to dance, and the chance to have Max by her side while she did it. Her two great loves, hand in hand.

"Yes, Max. This is what I wanted."

IT JUST ABOUT KILLED HIM, but he got through the evening and the next day, and he drove Maddy to the airport for her flight to Amsterdam that night.

He thought about flying with her, holding her hand through

the interview, but Maddy didn't need him for any of that. She knew how to dance without him.

He lay awake for a long time that night, aware of the space in the bed beside him.

Better get used to that, he told himself. *The sooner the better.*

She called from her hotel room the minute she got in from her interview the next day. He wiped the clay off his hands with a towel and held the phone to his ear with his shoulder as she raved about how nice everyone was and how much she loved the ethos of the new company and how excited she was about their ideas for shows and tours.

"They offered you a place, then?" he asked drily when he could get a word in edgeways.

"Yes! Yes! Didn't I mention that? God, I'm so excited I don't know whether to sit or do a handstand. Oh, Max, I wish you were here. We could go out and celebrate."

He dropped the towel and gripped the receiver.

"You'll have lots of things to sort out. Your apartment in Australia. You'll need to find a place in Amsterdam," he said.

"I know. They want to start rehearsals within the month. There's so much to sort out. Thank God for the Internet."

He took a deep breath. "I can get your gear together here, send it on. That will save you one trip and a bit of time, anyway," he said.

"Oh, no, I'll come back to Paris. I need to say goodbye to Eloise and Charlotte and talk to you. We need to plan your first visit to Amsterdam, Max," she said.

His grip tightened on the phone. "It's a nice idea, Maddy, but probably not a good one."

There was a short pause.

"Me coming back to Paris? Or you coming to Amsterdam?"

He could hear the hurt in her voice. He steeled himself. "Both, I guess."

"What about— What about us, Max?" she asked. Her voice was quiet and low. He imagined her sitting in her hotel room, her face crumpled with confusion.

But any hurt she was feeling would soon pass. She had a second chance at her career. The few weeks they'd had together would soon fade into insignificance as she lost herself in her craft again. If they'd ever had any significance in the first place. As Charlotte had so eloquently pointed out, Maddy needing him while he loved her was not a recipe for success. One of these things was definitely not like the other.

"I'll never forget it, Maddy. But we both know it only happened between us because of what was going on in your life. Let's quit while we're ahead," he said.

There was a long silence. He could hear her breathing on the other end of the phone.

"What about your sculptures? I mean, I'd like to know how you do with everything."

"Of course. I'll let you know if I ever get a show, send you pictures. You're my friend, Maddy. We'll always be friends."

Except it would kill him to see her, to talk to her, to hear about her life and how she was getting on without him. He'd do it, because he didn't want to hurt her and she would be hurt if he cut all contact. But he needed some time between now and whenever he next saw her to get his shit together. To find a way of surviving the next little while with this ache in his chest.

"I'll get your stuff together tomorrow and send it to you at the hotel," he said.

"Okay. Thanks."

She sounded as though she was crying. He closed his eyes and swore silently.

"I'll miss you, Max," she said.

"I'll miss you, too, Maddy."

There was nothing much else to say. He'd found a way for

Maddy to continue living her dream. Now he had to work out how to live his life without her in it.

He ended the call and stood staring at the phone for a long time. Then he walked to the kitchen and dug out the last bottle of cognac from his father's collection.

He poured himself a drink and took the bottle and the glass with him to the couch. Then he sat down and proceeded to get ball-tearingly wasted.

MADDY DIDN'T KNOW what to do with herself. She sat listening to the dial tone in her hotel room for a full five minutes before it occurred to her to hang up.

Max didn't want to see her again. He didn't even want her to come back to Paris to say goodbye properly. He'd just neatly excised her out of his life and waved *au revoir* without a backward glance.

She stood, then realized she had nowhere to go and sat again.

She simply hadn't expected it. She'd thought—she'd *assumed* that what she'd been feeling had been mutual. How could it not be, when her own feelings had been so all-encompassing and compelling?

But apparently not. Apparently Max had decided that their little fling had run its course. He'd found her this opportunity, and now he was going to pack her bags and send her off into the world, their liaison a thing of the past.

Was that all it had been, all it had meant? A liaison? A few weeks of sex between friends, no strings, no emotions, no consequences?

She put her head in her hands and pressed her fingertips to her forehead. How was it possible to feel so happy and so sad all at the same time? Max had found a way for her to dance again, but he'd also gently nudged her out of his apartment and out of his life. Time to move on, Maddy, he'd said in all but words.

I'll never forget it, Maddy. But we both know it only happened between us because of what was going on in your life.

What did that mean? That he'd been sleeping with her because she needed him? Because she'd been upset? Because she'd turned to him for comfort and, ever her friend, he'd given it?

Nausea swirled in her stomach as her memories of the past month were viewed through this new prism.

Max as her lover out of compassion. Max as her lover out of consideration and concern for a friend.

A sour taste filled her mouth. Surely not? Surely she hadn't fallen for him while he'd been *comforting* her?

Then she remembered the look in his eyes when he'd walked toward her sometimes, all hard body and harder erection, ready to claim what he wanted. And the times he'd thrown her onto the bed and made love to her with a greedy passion that had made her knees tremble and her insides melt.

Not a man acting out of friendship or concern. Max had wanted her. He'd said it himself, hadn't he? He'd always found her attractive. Always wanted to sleep with her.

Now he had. And, for him, their attraction had run its course. While for her, it had burgeoned into something far more profound and life-changing than mere sexual attraction.

She'd fallen in love with him, after ten years.

And he considered her nothing more than a friend.

She huffed out a humorless laugh. It figured that the only time she'd ever really, truly fallen in love she'd fallen for the one man who didn't want to make demands on her or wrest her away from her career. Far from it. Max didn't even care enough to make demands.

Like a child releasing a balloon, she let go of the idea, the hope that had been forming in her heart: a life with Max, good times shared with his family, standing proudly by Max's side as he sent his art out into the world, dancing knowing he was in the audience, watching her.

None of it would happen. She would never again have a chance to hold Eloise's warm, sweaty hands and look down into her joy-filled face as they danced together. She'd never again exasperate Charlotte with her failure to grasp the intricacies of handmade pastry. And she'd never wake up in Max's arms again, his body warm and hard against hers.

Dry-eyed, she crawled beneath the covers and pulled the blankets tight around herself.

Thank God she had her dancing, because she honestly did not know what she would do without it.

MAX FROWNED in irritation as he registered the knocking at his front door. He sighed heavily and abandoned the chisel and file he'd been working with to answer the summons.

Charlotte glowered at him when he flung it open.

"I've been knocking for ten minutes."

"I didn't hear you."

It was true. He'd been so absorbed in his work that he'd only registered the noise when he'd stepped back to check his progress.

Charlotte trailed after him as he returned to the five-foot-two-inch bronze figure poised beside his workbench. He was removing the marks from the sprues, the channels where the bronze had been poured into the mold made from his original clay sculpture. Two more bronze figures waited beside the first in various stages of completion.

He picked up his file, eyeing the shoulder he'd been working on. It still wasn't quite right....

Charlotte was huffing and puffing beside him as she surveyed his apartment. He didn't need to look to know what she was seeing: clothes piled on chairs, dishes overflowing the sink, newspapers in stacks near the door, take-out food containers and empty bottles of wine stacked beside the couch.

"You have to stop living like this. You're like a caveman. You only come out to get enough food to survive then you hole up back here in your apartment. When was the last time you shaved or did a load of laundry or changed your sheets?"

"Don't know. Don't care," he said, moving in to work on a molding mark.

"Will you stop that damned noise for five seconds and talk to me? I'm worried about you," Charlotte said.

He glanced across at her and saw how pale and tense she was.

"There's nothing to worry about. I'm fine. I'm working. I have a show in two weeks' time, in case you'd forgotten."

He still couldn't believe his luck. He'd been at the foundry supervising the casting of his second figure when Celeste Renou had seen his work. She owned a gallery in the exclusive Place des Vosges and had offered him a show on the spot.

He smiled grimly as he reflected that only Maddy's absence from his life had made it possible for him to come even close to making her deadline. He'd worked like a madman since the day Maddy left—morning, noon and night—channeling all his energy and regret and anger and frustration and lust and hurt and resentment into his art.

Three months. She'd been gone three months and he still woke to thoughts of her. He still smelled her perfume in his apartment, on his sheets and towels and shirts. He still found long strands of brown hair on his coat, his scarf.

He still loved her.

He was starting to wonder if that would ever change. Perhaps the best he could hope for was that his feelings would become dormant, as they had before. Lie down and play dead—until the next contact with Maddy, the next time he saw her or heard her voice.

"Max, this isn't about your show or your art or anything except for you. Have you looked in the mirror lately? You look like shit. You've lost weight. The homeless man on the corner has better personal hygiene. Talk to me."

"I'm fine."

"No, you're not. You're not over Maddy. You're not even close to being over Maddy, and I'm worried about what it's doing to you."

"I'll survive. The show will be over soon. I promise I'll shower before then."

She didn't smile. She looked as though she was struggling to contain herself.

"Okay, I'm going to say this because I think it needs to be said. You know I loved Maddy. I adored her. But the fact remains that she took off the moment she had a whiff of her career being resuscitated, and she didn't even bother to say goodbye to any of us. Including you. I'm sure she's had to learn to be so self-centered to survive in her profession, but it's not so great for everyone else in her life. Is she worth it, Max? I guess that's what I'm trying to ask you. Is Maddy worth all this angst and isolation?"

"Leave it, Charlotte."

"No. I think you need to hear this. While you're turning into a smelly crazy man, she's off dancing the light fantastic somewhere. Can't you see the imbalance? Can't you see—"

"It wasn't Maddy's fault, okay?" he snapped, unable to listen to his sister rail at Maddy when he knew the truth. He'd held his tongue through Charlotte's shock at Maddy's abrupt departure and Eloise's disappointment at losing her dancing teacher. He hadn't said a word. But for some reason, the closer the date for the opening of his show came, the more it chafed on him that he'd let his sister assume the worst about Maddy.

"Maddy didn't get a job offer and just take off. I found the opportunity for her through an old friend, set up an interview for her, encouraged her to go. And she wanted to come back to Paris to say goodbye, but I told her not to. So don't blame her if you're upset. Blame me."

Charlotte was openmouthed with shock.

"You *sent Maddy away?*" she said, her voice rising on a high note of incredulity.

"I found a way for her to dance again."

"In another country. And then you told her not to come back?" Charlotte's face was creased with confusion. "Why would you do that to yourself when you love her so much?"

He threw the file onto his workbench.

"You saw what she was like. She was brokenhearted about having to retire. I found her a second chance to do something she loved."

Charlotte sank into a chair. "My God. I always knew you had a Sir Galahad complex, but this takes the cake."

"I wanted her to be happy," he said defensively.

"I got that, you noble idiot. Did you at least tell her how you felt before she left?"

He looked at her but said nothing.

Charlotte swore loud and long. "Max! Are you telling me you packed Maddy off and you never said a word to her about how you feel?"

His continued silence was answer enough. Charlotte shot to her feet, throwing her hands in the air in exasperation.

"All this time I've been angry with Maddy for abandoning you, and she was the one I should have felt sorry for. Why didn't you say something to her before she left, Max?"

"There was no point."

"Why?"

"Because I know how she feels. I've always known how she feels."

Charlotte closed her eyes and made a sound like a kettle boiling. "You are such a...man!"

"What's that supposed to mean?"

"You have no idea how Maddy feels."

"I've known her for ten years. I know exactly how she feels."

"No, you don't. You think you know, but you don't, because you never asked her. You never told her how you feel, and you never asked her how she feels."

"It wouldn't have made any difference," he said stubbornly.

Charlotte stepped close and grabbed his arm, her eyes intense as they bored into him. "You don't know that."

He stared at her, and she shook his arm.

"You sent her to Amsterdam without telling her you didn't want her to go. How do you think she must have felt, Max? First you find her a job thousands of miles away, then you drive her to the airport and tell her not to bother coming back. My God. Even if she didn't love you she must have felt as though she'd overstayed her welcome."

For the first time he considered what had happened from Maddy's point of view. She'd been thrilled about the new role with the Nederlands Dans Theatre. He knew he was right about that. But she'd spoken about him visiting her in Amsterdam. And she'd wanted to come back to Paris to sort things out with him.

What if his sister was right? What if he'd pushed Maddy away when he should have been pulling her close? What if he'd been so busy giving her what he thought she wanted and protecting himself that he'd destroyed his one chance at happiness?

"I've spent so long believing it would never happen between us I couldn't see any other way forward," he finally admitted.

"Call her."

He shook his head. There were things he needed to say that couldn't be said over a phone. He needed to see her in person, to look into her eyes.

"She's coming for the show at the end of the month," he said.

"You could fly over and see her before then. After you spend about a week in the shower detoxing and de-fleaing yourself."

"No."

An idea was forming. He reached for his diary, flicking through the pages. There was almost enough time. Hell, he'd make the time if he had to.

"Max..."

"No. There's something I want to do first. Something I need to do," he said.

It was an idea he'd had for a while, something that had been tickling at the back of his mind ever since he finished the last model for his full-size bronzes. A smaller piece. An intensely personal, private piece to complete the series.

He crossed to his workbench, started assembling the materials he'd need.

"Here we go. The mad genius at work," Charlotte said.

He barely heard her. He was too gripped by what he needed to do. Somehow, he needed to show Maddy how he felt, to make her understand. If he was going to declare himself, he was going to do it right.

MADDY CHECKED her lipstick for the fourth time as the taxi turned into the narrow streets leading to Place de Vosges. She was nervous. No point kidding herself. She had no idea how she was going to handle seeing Max again.

She'd spoken to him exactly three times since the night he'd told her not to return to Paris. He'd called to let her know when her things would be arriving, then she'd called him to ask about Eloise, concerned the little girl was missing her dancing lessons. She needn't have bothered—Max had already stepped in to take her place and he'd reported Eloise was thriving.

The last time they'd spoken he'd invited her to his show. It had been awkward between them. She hadn't known what to ask, where to start. The same question kept bubbling up inside her, begging for release.

Did it mean so little to you? Do I mean so little to you?

She tightened her grip on her purse as the cab rolled to a stop. She'd already pulled a twenty-euro note from her wallet and she handed it over then slid from the car.

Warm spring air danced around her calves as she slowly walked along the elegant, covered walkway of Place des Vosges. More than any other part of Paris it reminded her of the Hollywood ideal of a European setting—a huge square bordered on four sides by identical brick buildings, all uniformly five stories high, all in red brick. The square in the middle had been nothing but gravel and stark, bare trees when she left. Tonight, it was filled with Parisians enjoying the warm weather, picnicking on the grass, studying, kissing, laughing beneath arching green trees.

She hadn't realized how much she'd missed Paris until the taxi had hit the old center and she'd caught her first glimpse of cobblestones. Max lived here. That was why she loved it. Paris was the city where she'd fallen in love.

There were several galleries facing the Place des Vosges, but only one was filled with elegantly dressed people sipping champagne.

Max's opening. She was full of so many different emotions she felt she might overflow. Pride, love, hurt—she didn't know where one ended and the other began.

Her high heels tapped on the stone walkway as she made her way to the gallery entrance. She couldn't see anyone she knew—Charlotte, Richard, Max—and she tried to calm herself. The gallery interior was stark white with high arched ceilings, all the better to show off the art, she guessed. There were so many people present she couldn't see Max's work, and she started to move into the crowd, determined to see at last the fruits of their time together.

She'd sat for him for hours in the end. When he told her he'd been offered a show, she'd wondered what his work would be like. If he had used her as his model, or if he'd found someone else. Yvette, or another dancer.

"Maddy. There you are!"

She turned to see Charlotte bearing down on her, arms wide, a glass of champagne in one hand.

"You look gorgeous, as always," Charlotte said, holding Maddy's hands out to the side so she could inspect her deep red velvet sheath.

"That can only be French," she said with a knowing eye.

Maddy smiled. "Actually, it's Italian," she said.

Charlotte pulled a face. "We'll keep it quiet, no one will know."

Maddy's eyes slid over her shoulder, searching the crowd.

"He's toward the back. We both saw you arrive but he's stuck with some boring arts patron who keeps fondling Max's arm like a pet dog or something," Charlotte said.

"Oh."

"Ah. Here he is now."

Maddy swiveled on her heel, her heart in her throat, her palms suddenly sweaty.

Her eyes ate him up, taking in his elegantly messy hair, the sharp lines of his face, the crispness of his white shirt and midnight-navy suit. Cuff links glinted at his wrists and his shoulders looked impossibly wide.

"Maddy," he said.

His gaze scanned her face intently before finally his eyes locked with hers and they were staring at each other for the first time in three months.

A deluge of memories hit her: Max looking into her eyes as he made love to her in the shower, Max laughing at her disastrous attempts at cooking, the solemn watchfulness on his face as he'd told her about the opportunity in Amsterdam.

"You look beautiful," he said.

Heat raced up her spine as his gaze skimmed over her breasts and down her waist. She still found him enormously attractive, even though they were only supposed to be friends now.

Not for the first time, she wondered how she would survive tonight with her pride intact. How was she going to stop herself from telling him how she felt, what she wanted?

"This is a wonderful turnout," she said because she couldn't think of anything else to say. "You must be pleased."

He shrugged. "I've been waiting for you to get here."

Another wave of heat raced up her spine.

Don't get carried away, Maddy. He's just being friendly.

But there was something in his manner, the way he reached for her hand, the way he hesitated before threading his fingers through hers.

"There's something I want to show you," he said.

He led her deeper into the gallery, towing her behind him. She studied the strong column of his neck, the white collar of his shirt. Her gaze dipped to his backside, remembering the flex and contract of his hard muscles as he pumped into her. Her breath caught in her throat and her hand twitched in his.

Suddenly she was filled with an intense longing. She wanted things to be the way they had been during those magical few weeks in Max's apartment. Even in the midst of her grief over losing her career, she'd never been happier. And now she had her career but no Max. She knew which state she preferred, which grief was surmountable and which was not.

The crowd parted before Max, people smiling and watching him avidly as he passed. Without even seeing his work Maddy understood that he was a hit. People watched him as if he was a star, a somebody.

Then a man stepped to one side and she saw the first sculpture—a ballerina arching forward in a perfect arabesque, the muscles of her slim frame straining. Her face was lifted, her expression serene, as though she was exactly where she needed to be.

The detail in the piece was extraordinary—the curve of the dancer's naked breasts, the texture of curls between her thighs, the hollow beneath her armpit, the lines around her mouth and eyes. For a second Maddy fell victim to a wave of acute self-consciousness. This was her naked body, her face, depicted so faithfully, in such detail. This was so much more than what she'd imagined when she'd agreed to model for Max. He'd captured her forever. And then the self-consciousness was washed away as awe at his skill, at his power, swept over her.

"She's beautiful," she said, overwhelmed by Max's talent. "I almost feel as though she's about to move."

"She's you, Maddy," he said quietly. He tugged on her hand. "There's more."

He led her to the next dancer, caught forever in the middle of a pirouette. Maddy looked into her own face, cast in bronze, the expression there a mixture of pain and joy.

"Do I really look like that when I dance?" she asked him.

"Yes. When you danced for me."

The next figure was a dying swan, the dancer languishing at their feet in despair. Then there was a dancer executing a grand plié, and finally a seated posture, the ballerina contemplating her sore feet as she slipped off her shoes in a quiet moment.

"Well, those are definitely my bent toes," she said drily. "When did you do this sketch?"

"When you weren't looking. I wanted a quiet, private moment."

He'd found it. She was blown away by the beauty and energy and fineness of his work. Blown away, also, by the fact that all the dancers were her. He hadn't used Yvette or anyone else.

Max was watching her expectantly and she realized that there was one last sculpture remaining, a smaller figure placed beyond the adult dancers.

She took a step forward. Then her hand went to her mouth as she understood what she was looking at.

A little girl stood there, one hand on the barre, her feet turned out, the other hand raised over her head in a graceful arc. The little girl's head was tilted so she could follow the line of her raised hand with her eyes, and the look on her face was pure joy, the expression of a little soul who had found her calling in life.

Maddy's eyes filled with tears.

"I thought I was finished when I'd cast the first six. But then I realized that I wasn't," he said.

"How did you…?" The resemblance to her four-year-old self was uncanny.

"You had a picture in your room a long time ago," he said.

"And you remembered?"

He nodded. She studied the figure and a slow understanding dawned on her.

She saw the deep, abiding love that was evident in every line of the figure and the hollowness that she'd carried inside her for three months evaporated as she turned to look at Max. He couldn't have made this sculpture and not feel something more than friendship for her. It simply wasn't possible. Surely…?

He was holding something in his hands, and she frowned as she recognized it.

"My scarf," she said stupidly.

"Maddy, I've been wanting to say this to you for a long time. Ten years, in fact. I love you. I've loved you from the moment I met you. I've loved you every minute since. This scarf…well, frankly, I stole it so I could have something to remember you by. But I'm giving it back tonight because I'd rather have you."

For a moment all she could do was stare at him. What he

was saying changed her world. Changed everything. Their shared history. Her present. Her future. She blinked, trying to come to terms with what she'd just heard.

Max had always loved her. Always. When they were living together. When they were dancing together. When he was offering her comfort and solace.

All that time he'd loved her.

Suddenly she noticed how tight his jaw was, how square his shoulders were. Tension emanated from every muscle. He was waiting for her, waiting for her reaction. She didn't know whether to laugh or cry she was so touched by how uncertain he was.

"Max," she said. She had no words for the feeling expanding in her chest. Shaking her head at her inability to articulate her emotions, she settled for reaching up and holding his face as she stood on her tiptoes and kissed him. His hands found her face, and they pressed their mouths together in an intense, fierce meeting of souls.

Finally she broke the kiss and looked up into his face, just inches from hers.

"Max, I love you, too. I've spent the past three months living without you and I never want to be that unhappy again in my life."

For a heartbeat Max stared into her face. She saw how deep the doubt went in him, and it almost broke her heart as she understood how hard it must have been for him to love her for so long without any acknowledgment from her.

Then his eyes cleared and a smile tugged at the corners of his mouth.

"Maddy," he said. He kissed her, his tongue sliding into her mouth, his body pressing against hers, his hands sliding into her hair to hold her steady so he could drink his fill of her.

They broke the kiss to stare at each other again. Maddy found herself smiling the same goofy, slightly bemused smile that Max was smiling.

"I thought you sent me away because you were sick of me," she said.

"I sent you away because I wanted you to be happy, to have what you wanted," he said.

"I wanted you. Only you. The chance to dance again was a nice surprise, a lovely chance for me to say goodbye to a part of my life. But you're my future, Max."

His smile broadened into a grin as he absorbed her words and he pulled her into his arms, lifted her and spun her in a circle. He was about to kiss her again when the sound of a clearing throat alerted them to the fact that they had an audience.

They glanced up, registering for the first time the circle of interested art lovers surrounding them. Charlotte stepped forward, one eyebrow raised.

"I think the Americans have a phrase for this, yes?" she said. "Get a room? Is that it?"

Max threw back his head and laughed. It was the best sound Maddy had ever heard in her life, but suddenly tears were squeezing from beneath her eyelids and running down her face. Max's smile faded and he reached out to cup her cheek.

"Maddy, don't cry," he said, his face a picture of dismay.

"I'm so sorry," she said. "I'm so sorry for not understanding sooner. For not seeing. All those times I climbed into your bed. All those times I bitched to you about my boyfriends…"

He shook his head and pressed his fingers to her lips.

"No. No looking back."

"But—"

"No. From this moment on there is only now, and tomorrow. Nothing else matters."

He started pulling her toward the front of the gallery. A tall white-haired woman intercepted them.

"Max! Where are you going?" she asked, eyebrows disappearing into her white hair.

"I need to consult with my muse," he said.

The woman looked outraged. "Now? You need to consult with your muse now?"

Max shot Maddy a dirty, dirty look.

"Definitely. And at great length."

He pulled Maddy out into the street.

"Who was that?" she asked.

He shrugged. "Gallery owner."

"Oh my God."

She pulled her hand free and raced back to the gallery entrance. "We'll be back. Half an hour." She thought again, remembering what it was like when she and Max were skin to skin, how crazy they got. "An hour, tops."

Max slid his arms around her and kissed her soundly when she rejoined him. She could feel how hard he was, his erection pressing against her belly. She was so ready for him she wanted to pull him into a doorway and have her wicked way with him on the spot.

"An hour?" he said. "I'm going to need more than an hour to show you how much I love you, Maddy."

"I know. But we've got the rest of our lives, right?"

He stared into her face, his fingers curling possessively into her hips.

"Yes. We have forever."

Then he took her home.

SIX MONTHS LATER, Maddy stood in the wings and waited for her musical cue. Through a gap in the curtain she could see a sliver of the audience in the stalls and the dim shadow of the dress circle in the background. She lifted her gaze to Chagall's roof, savoring the sight, the moment.

It felt absolutely right that her last performance as a prima ballerina should be here at the Opera Garnier. Paris was her home now. And this was a special place, a fitting place to draw the line under her career.

She would miss performances like this one. A part of her would always grieve the end of her career. But she had new things to look forward to in life. Dancing wasn't her earth, moon and stars anymore.

She smiled as she thought of Max, her husband now for all of a month. His would be one of the first faces she saw when she took to the stage, sitting front row center.

She took a deep breath. She loved him so much. More every day.

He'd sold every piece from his debut exhibition and was working on a second show. They'd moved to a new apartment two months ago, hanging on to his old one so he could convert it into his atelier. It was going to be tough for the next few years, financially speaking, but she had every confidence that Max was going to have a great art career.

She was looking forward to modeling for him again, in between her new studies at the Sorbonne. She was training to become a dance therapist. Her work with Eloise had shown her that there were many different ways to weave dancing into her life and she planned to specialize in working with autistic children if she could. The idea of going back to school after so many years away was frankly terrifying, but she was determined to rise to the occasion. She knew how to work hard, after all. Hopefully the rest would follow.

She stepped back from the curtain as the music swelled. It was time to say goodbye.

She found her starting point, took a deep belly breath…

And then she was on the stage, defying gravity, doing the thing she loved, had always loved. She savored each pirouette, every arabesque. Her last performance. Her swan song, her goodbye to her first love.

In the audience, she caught sight of Max's face. She could see his pride, see the tears shimmering in his eyes.

Her heart lifting, she gave herself over to the music and danced.

* * * * *

Here's a sneak peek at
THE CEO'S CHRISTMAS PROPOSITION,
the first in USA TODAY *bestselling author*
Merline Lovelace's HOLIDAYS ABROAD *trilogy*
coming in November 2008.

American Devon McShay is about to get the Christmas surprise of a lifetime when she meets her new client, sexy billionaire Caleb Logan, for the very first time.

Silhouette Desire

Available November 2008

Her breath whistled out in a sigh of relief when he exited Customs. Devon recognized him right away from the newspaper and magazine articles her friend and partner Sabrina had looked up during her frantic prep work.

Caleb John Logan, Jr. Thirty-one. Six-two. With jet-black hair, laser-blue eyes and a linebacker's shoulders under his charcoal-gray cashmere overcoat. His jaw-dropping good looks didn't score him any points with Devon. She'd learned the hard way not to trust handsome heartbreakers like Cal Logan.

But he was a client. An important one. And she was willing to give someone who'd served a hitch in the marines before earning a B.S. from the University of Oregon, an MBA from Stanford and his first million at the ripe old age of twenty-six the benefit of the doubt.

Right up until he spotted the hot-pink pashmina, that is.

Devon knew the flash of color was more visible than the sign she held up with his name on it. So she wasn't surprised when Logan picked her out of the crowd and cut in her direction. She'd just plastered on her best businesswoman smile when he whipped an arm around her waist. The next moment she was sprawled against his cashmere-covered chest.

"Hello, brown eyes."

Swooping down, he covered her mouth with his.

Sheer astonishment kept Devon rooted to the spot for a few seconds while her mind whirled chaotically. Her first thought was that her client had downed a few too many drinks during the long flight. Her second, that he'd mistaken the kind of escort and consulting services her company provided. Her third shoved everything else out of her head.

The man could kiss!

His mouth moved over hers with a skill that ignited sparks at a half dozen flash points throughout her body. Devon hadn't experienced that kind of spontaneous combustion in a while. A *long* while.

The sparks were still popping when she pushed off his chest, only now they fueled a flush of anger.

"Do you always greet women you don't know with a liplock, Mr. Logan?"

A smile crinkled the skin at the corners of his eyes. "As a matter of fact, I don't. That was from Don."

"Huh?"

"He said he owed you one from New Year's Eve two years ago and made me promise to deliver it."

She stared up at him in total incomprehension. Logan hooked a brow and attempted to prompt a nonexistent memory.

"He abandoned you at the Waldorf. Five minutes before midnight. To deliver twins."

"I don't have a clue who or what you're..."

Understanding burst like a water balloon.

"Wait a sec. Are you talking about Sabrina's old boyfriend? Your buddy, who's now an ob-gyn doc?"

It was Logan's turn to look startled. He recovered faster than Devon had, though. His smile widened into a rueful grin.

"I take it you're not Sabrina Russo."

"No, Mr. Logan, I am *not*."

* * * * *

Be sure to look for
THE CEO'S CHRISTMAS PROPOSITION
by Merline Lovelace.
Available in November 2008 wherever books are sold,
including most bookstores, supermarkets,
drugstores and discount stores.

Silhouette Desire

MERLINE LOVELACE

THE CEO'S CHRISTMAS PROPOSITION

After being stranded in Austria together at Christmas, it takes only one kiss for aerospace CEO Cal Logan to decide he wants more than just a business relationship with Devon McShay. But when Cal's credibility is questioned, he has to fight to clear his name, and to get Devon to trust her heart.

Available November wherever books are sold.

Holidays Abroad

Always Powerful, Passionate and Provocative.

Visit Silhouette Books at www.eHarlequin.com

HARLEQUIN Blaze

Travel back to Skull Creek, Texas—
where all the best-looking men
are cowboys, and some of those
cowboys are *vampires!*

USA TODAY bestselling author
Kimberly Raye ties up her
Love at First Bite trilogy with...

A BODY TO DIE FOR

Vampire Viviana Darland is in Skull Creek, Texas, looking for one thing—an orgasm. Or more specifically, the only man who'd ever given her one, vampire Garret Sawyer. She knows her end is near, and wants one good climax before she goes. And she intends to get it—before Garret delivers on his promise to kill her....

Paranormal adventure at its sexiest!

Available in November 2008 wherever
Harlequin Blaze books are sold.

www.eHarlequin.com

REQUEST YOUR FREE BOOKS!

2 FREE NOVELS PLUS 2 FREE GIFTS!

HARLEQUIN® Blaze™

Red-hot reads!

YES! Please send me 2 FREE Harlequin® Blaze™ novels and my 2 FREE gifts (gifts are worth about $10). After receiving them, if I don't wish to receive any more books, I can return the shipping statement marked "cancel." If I don't cancel, I will receive 6 brand-new novels every month and be billed just $4.24 per book in the U.S. or $4.71 per book in Canada, plus 25¢ shipping and handling per book and applicable taxes, if any*. That's a savings of 15% or more off the cover price! I understand that accepting the 2 free books and gifts places me under no obligation to buy anything. I can always return a shipment and cancel at any time. Even if I never buy another book, the two free books and gifts are mine to keep forever.

151 HDN ERVA   351 HDN ERUX

Name _____ (PLEASE PRINT) _____

Address _____ Apt. # _____

City _____ State/Prov. _____ Zip/Postal Code _____

Signature (if under 18, a parent or guardian must sign) _____

Mail to the **Harlequin Reader Service**:
IN U.S.A.: P.O. Box 1867, Buffalo, NY 14240-1867
IN CANADA: P.O. Box 609, Fort Erie, Ontario L2A 5X3

Not valid to current subscribers of Harlequin Blaze books.

Want to try two free books from another line?
Call 1-800-873-8635 or visit www.morefreebooks.com.

* Terms and prices subject to change without notice. N.Y. residents add applicable sales tax. Canadian residents will be charged applicable provincial taxes and GST. Offer not valid in Quebec. This offer is limited to one order per household. All orders subject to approval. Credit or debit balances in a customer's account(s) may be offset by any other outstanding balance owed by or to the customer. Please allow 4 to 6 weeks for delivery. Offer available while quantities last.

Your Privacy: Harlequin Books is committed to protecting your privacy. Our Privacy Policy is available online at www.eHarlequin.com or upon request from the Reader Service. From time to time we make our lists of customers available to reputable third parties who have a product or service of interest to you. If you would prefer we not share your name and address, please check here. ☐

HB08R

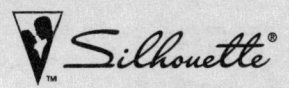

Silhouette®
Romantic SUSPENSE
Sparked by Danger, Fueled by Passion.

Lindsay McKenna
Susan Grant

Mission: Christmas

Celebrate the holidays with a pair of military heroines and their daring men in two romantic, adventurous stories from these bestselling authors.

Featuring:

"The Christmas Wild Bunch"
by *USA TODAY* bestselling author
Lindsay McKenna

and

"Snowbound with a Prince"
by *New York Times* bestselling author
Susan Grant

Available November wherever books are sold.

HARLEQUIN Blaze

COMING NEXT MONTH

#429 KISS & TELL Alison Kent
In the world of celebrity tabloids, Caleb MacGregor is the best. Once he smells a scandal, he makes sure the world knows. And that's exactly what Miranda Kelly is afraid of. Hiding behind her stage name, Miranda hopes she'll avoid his notice. And she does—until she invites Caleb into her bed.

#430 UNLEASHED Lori Borrill
It's a wild ride in more ways than one when Jessica Beane is corralled into a road trip by homicide detective Rick Marshall. Crucial evidence is missing and Jess is the key to unlocking not just the case, but their pent-up passion, as well!

#431 A BODY TO DIE FOR Kimberly Raye
Love at First Bite, Bk. 3
Vampire Viviana Darland is in Skull Creek, Texas, looking for one thing—an orgasm. Or more specifically, the only man who's ever given her one, vampire Garret Sawyer. She knows her end is near, and wants one good climax before she goes. And she intends to get it—before Garret delivers on his promise to kill her....

#432 HER SEXIEST SURPRISE Dawn Atkins
He's the best birthday gift ever! When Chloe Baxter makes a sexy wish on her birthday candles, she never expects Riley Connelly—her secret crush—to appear. Nor does she expect him to give her the hottest night of her life. It's so hot, why share just one night?

#433 RECKLESS Tori Carrington
Indecent Proposals, Bk. 1
Heidi Joblowski isn't a woman to leave her life to chance. Her plan? To marry her perfect boyfriend, Jesse, and have several perfect children. Unfortunately, the only perfect thing in her life lately is the sex she's been having with Jesse's best friend Kyle....

#434 IN A BIND Stephanie Bond
Sex for Beginners, Bk. 2
Flight attendant Zoe Smythe is working her last shift, planning her wedding... and doing her best to ignore the sexual chemistry between her and a seriously sexy Australian passenger. But when she reads a letter she'd written in college, reminding her of her most private, erotic fantasies...all bets are off!

www.eHarlequin.com